D0399186

THE
DEATH-DEFYING
PEPPER ROUX

OTHER BOOKS BY
GERALDINE McCAUGHREAN

THE
DEATH-DEFYING
PEPPER ROUX

GERALDINE
McCAUGHREAN

HARPER

An Imprint of HarperCollinsPublishers
HILLSBORO PUBLIC LIBRARIES
Hillsboro, OR
Member of Washington County
COOPERATIVE LIBRARY SERVICES

ACKNOWLEDGMENTS

Let me thank, in England, Ron for liking it,
Liz for taking it, Kate for checking it, Ailsa for sharing it,
and John for the bits about boats.

As to the crew in America,
I must especially thank Renée for doing more
with a pencil than even Pepper could have dreamed . . .
and Catherine for being everlastingly fourteen.

Library of Congress Cataloging-in-Publication Data
McCaughrean, Geraldine.
    The death-defying Pepper Roux / Geraldine McCaughrean.
        p.   cm.
    Summary: Having been raised believing he will die before he reaches the age of fourteen,
Pepper Roux runs away on his fourteenth birthday in an attempt to elude his fate, assumes another
identity, and continues to try to outrun death, no matter the consequences. 4261   8107
    ISBN 978-0-06-183665-7 (trade bdg.) — ISBN 978-0-06-183666-4 (lib. bdg.)   410
    [1. Adventure and adventurers—Fiction.   2. Disguise—Fiction.   3. Survival—Fiction.
4. Fate and fatalism—Fiction.   5. France—History—20th century—Fiction.]   I. Title.
PZ7.M4784133De   2010   2009039665
[Fic]—dc22   CIP
                                                                                   AC

Typography by Ray Shappell
10 11 12 13 14   LP/RRDB   10 9 8 7 6 5 4 3 2 1
❖
First U.S. Edition, 2010
Originally published in 2009 in the U.K. by Oxford University Press

For Catherine Onder with love

CONTENTS

ONE

BIRTHDAY BOY

On the morning of his fourteenth birthday, Pepper had been awake for fully two minutes before realizing it was the day he must die. His heart cannoned like a billiard ball off some soft green wall of his innards. This had to be the day everyone had been waiting for—and he was terrified he would disappoint them, make a poor showing, let people down.

His mother's face, when he entered the breakfast room, was ashen. He could not bring himself to meet her big-eyed, tear-brimming gaze, though he felt it follow him to the scrambled eggs and the cold ham. She never kissed him in the mornings. In fact she never kissed him at all. Aunt Mireille had said his parents should not become too fond of *"le pauvre"*—poor thing—if they were to cope with the grief of losing him.

Pepper's real name was Paul, but when he was small and people asked him, he told them it was Pauvre. After all, that was the name his mother had always used. "Get dressed, *mon pauvre.*" "Eat up, *mon pauvre.*" "Say good-bye, *pauvre petit.*" His little comrades at school were confused and called him "Poivre," and their mothers asked, "Pepper? Why is the child called Pepper?"

It was all Aunt Mireille's fault. Unmarried Aunt Mireille lodged with her married sister. So when Madame Roux gave birth to a lovely little boy, Aunt Mireille was first to be introduced. Leaning over the cot, she sucked on her big yellow teeth and said, with a tremor in her voice, "To think he'll be dead by fourteen, *le pauvre.*"

"No!" exclaimed Pepper's poor mother. "Why would you say such a thing?"

"It is the Lord's will, I'm afraid, dear," whispered the devout Aunt Mireille. "Saint Constance told me so in a dream last night." She dropped this bad news into the crib like a teething ring, a little christening gift: Pepper would be dead before he was full-grown.

With the man of the house away at sea, the women leaned against each other and complained about the unfairness of life. In fact the two of them leaned in against Pepper's childhood like a pair of bookends—big, ponderous women, and so full of tragedy that they could barely hook their corsets closed. For his first birthday, Aunt Mireille bought *le pauvre* a charming little plot in the churchyard just the right size for a small grave.

Pepper did not question his doom, any more than he would have questioned having asthma or knock-knees. Saint Constance knew, and he accepted it. He was a sturdy, healthy boy, but his mother treated him like an invalid, feeding him calf's-foot jelly from a spoon and tea brewed from weeds in the garden. Instead of finger rhymes, his aunty taught him the last rites, tugging each of his tiny fingers when the responses should come. Instead of lullabies, she taught him psalms about bones wasting away, foes with gnashing teeth, and the valley of the shadow of Death.

The only taste he got of manliness was when his father came home fleetingly between voyages. Captain Roux served the boy glasses of rum neat (then drank

them himself) and took Pepper to see unsuitable melo-
dramas. He brought home the seeds of exotic foreign
fruits, and together father and son planted them outside the north-facing windows. The seedlings (like
Pepper) were not really expected to grow to any size
before they died.

An expensive education seemed pointless. Besides,
his mother wanted to make the most of him, so after
primary school had taught him to read and write, she
kept him at home, where the estate hands thought the
young master must be feebleminded and were very
sorry (but not for Pepper).

He stood on tiptoe to reach as much education as he
could from his father's bookshelves, which were particularly rich in pirates, knots, and things nautical. So
he brightened the dullness of his days with imaginary
trips to the Cape of Good Hope, the Caribbees, and
the Barbary Coast. His pretend ship was the family
winepress. It rarely held anything but leftover wine
fumes, and he climbed out, head reeling, feeling quite
as sick as if he had really been to sea. But since the
only people he ever met were pious, proper visitors to
the house, he supposed even pirates must be pious and

proper too. The ones in his imagination took tea in the afternoon.

And never got killed.

The days clattered down like rows of dominoes. Pepper's voice broke and so did his mother's heart, knowing "The Time" must be near. She bit her lip and prayed for her boy's end to come painlessly, without suffering. Aunt Mireille, though, was more practical. She rehearsed him in what to say when he reached Paradise: greetings and messages for him to deliver when he met up with the Blessed Dead. When he failed to learn them, she took to pushing slips of paper into his pockets and up the cuffs of his nightshirt—"Now be sure to give this to Aunt Félice, won't you, child? And this to Father Michel." There would be other notes when he went up to bed, pinned to his bedhead with sewing needles or brooches:

Kindly pray for us sinners now and at the hour of our death.

Your obedient servant,
Mireille Lepont (Miss)

5

Pepper himself took to climbing to the top of anything tall—hills, trees, roofs—to see if Death was riding toward him on a white horse, under a black banner or preceded by a pillar of fire. He scanned the sky for angels sitting on the clouds, fishing for souls with fishing rods; for fiery chariots descending to kidnap him. Heights did not frighten him. After years of wondering how he would die—comparing the options, as it were—he had decided that falling would be best: It would feel quite like flying on the way down, and the pain would be quickly over. Not that he would get to choose. Childhood was a mousetrap from which he could never expect to escape. The world was something happening to other people—people with destinations other than a plot in the graveyard. So Pepper perched, like a migratory bird on a twig, waiting for winter.

But winter did not come.

His aunt treated him more and more coldly, like a guest who has outstayed his welcome. Even his father found him a sort of embarrassment—"What, you still here, boy?"—when he came home between voyages.

"I'm sorry, Papa."

"Are you sure you didn't mishear, Mireille?" the

captain snapped at his sister-in-law. "Mistake fourteen for forty? Easy mistake. Fourteen. Forty."

Pepper was so taken with this idea that he leaped upright in his chair and knocked over a glass of water, which swamped his aunt's bread plate.

No, Mireille assured them, poking her wet bread disgustedly with a fork: Saint Constance had very good diction and formed all her words beautifully. She had definitely said Pepper would be dead by the time he was fourteen. "In fact . . . ," said Mireille, remembering to mention it for the first time, "in fact, she has repeated it to me on several occasions. *Fourteen*."

To escape their reproach, Pepper took himself off into the fields and shot inanimate objects with his father's pistol. He had no taste for shooting live things, like rats or pigeons: He felt too much in common with them, being short-lived and a bit of a nuisance himself. He would have liked to shoot all the wretched rooks that were plaguing the estate. Aunt Mireille promised that "birds of ill omen" would "gather overhead when The Hour has come." But he supposed it was unkind to shoot the birds just because they wore funeral black.

* * *

"We thought a trip to church and then a walk as far as the river," said Aunt Mireille, as Pepper sat down to his last breakfast.

"I went to confession yesterday," he said.

"Can we go on our knees too often before the throne of God?" inquired Mireille in a whisper, as though she were already in church. Pepper was tempted to say that yes, he thought one probably could. His kneecaps had large ugly calluses on them from kneeling to pray. What maiden would ever look kindly upon such knee-caps? Aunt Mireille frequently told him to loathe his mortal flesh. But Pepper could only manage to loathe his knees. The rest of him he was secretly rather fond of. Like a beautiful watch, it might not go for long without stopping, but it was pretty even so.

A silence fell then over the breakfast table; a silence so intense that Pepper was embarrassed by the sound of his chewing and felt obliged to stop. His stomach gurgled cheerfully, showing too little respect for the occasion. His mother unfolded a letter and was going to read it aloud when she suddenly rounded her shoulders and started weeping. It did not matter. He knew the letter already; she had read it to him many times before. It was his father's farewell:

"Let go ropes, then. Raise sail. Fair winds.
Safe harbors. Worse things happen to others.
These things are sent to test us. Bear up.
Do not reproach yourself on my account.
It could not be helped, I daresay. The world
goes along. I am not a carping man. I remain . . ."

Yes, you do, don't you? thought Pepper with uncharacteristic bitterness. *You remain.*

"Your loving Father,
Gilbert Roux (Captain)"

"I was hoping your dear father would be here!" his mother sobbed. "Pray God he has not had the misfortune to sink again! Elsewise, surely he would have come to help us through!"

Aunt Mireille snorted, partly out of contempt for Captain Roux's rather accident-prone career, partly as if to imply, *When are men ever in the right place at the right time?*

"I thought I might go into town," said Pepper. "Just me."

"Oh, but son!"

Aunt Mireille laid a soothing hand on her sister's arm. "If that's what *le pauvre* wishes," she said, as if she knew more than she was saying. Perhaps Saint Constance had revealed to her how Pepper was going to die! Something townish, involving falling buildings? Pepper knew he should not try to thwart Fate, but thought he might stay home after all.

The room, though, seemed to be getting smaller and smaller—shrinking to the size and shape of a coffin. The smell of the women was stronger than the breakfast kedgeree: Parma violets and lavender water. The flies in the center of the ceiling went around and around: They ought to spread out to the cobwebbed corners, and get caught and die. Why should they escape when he could not?

He could feel himself smothering, got up, and went to the door for some air. As he opened it, the sunlight came in like a battering ram. Would Death come in like that, or was it waiting for him somewhere outside?

Pepper looked back at the two great gray women seated at the table, Aunt Mireille searching in her bag for nail scissors—what for? To cut his life's thread herself? On an impulse, he stepped out into the yard in his shirtsleeves and started walking, and kept walking until he reached the road.

He walked toward the sea.

In the trees—in every tree—the rooks were stirring, rising into the sky, but sinking back again onto their roosts. It was still too early for them to venture out onto the flat fields. So the sunny, clumping crowns of the elms swarmed with blackness, like heads teeming with lice. The birds' noise was horrific—a rending, ranting madness very like the feeling in Pepper's chest. Birds of ill omen, of course. More than ever. They must have sent for reinforcements to help batter home his doom: *Warned you! Warned you! Die, boy! Die!*

The only trees with no rookeries in them were the masts of two ships docked in the harbor. Not until Pepper reached the head of the bay could he see the funnels too, and then the steamers they belonged to, cradled in the embrace of the harbor wall. One was his father's.

At first he thought he must be mistaken—how different could one coastal steamship look from another, after all? But no: It truly was *La Berenice*, showing all the scuffs and scars of a ship that has been too long on the water. She was aswarm with men stripping her fittings, clearing her decks.

"Refit," said a sailor untangling and coiling ropes onshore—and then (because he was a man of few words), "Refitting."

"Where's Captain Roux?" asked Pepper. "Where's the master?"

"Get away, boy!" said the man unexpectedly. He might almost have been some old prophet warning of flood or pestilence: *Get away!* But he simply meant that Pepper was standing on a tangle of rope, stopping his work. "Shift yourself, lad."

Pepper stepped back. He ran his eyes over his father's ship. Clearly *La Berenice* had been moored for days. So why had his father not appeared at home? Where had he gone instead?

"Hotel," said the man of few words.

"Ah."

"Find him there."

But Pepper was content to have solved the mystery. His father had docked but preferred not to return home until *after* his son's fatal fourteenth birthday. Did not want to be "in at the death," so to speak.

"Get away!" said the man of few words.

Again it sounded prophetic. But it was not. The sailor had just glanced up at the masthead and seen a carpenter lose his grip on a big oak pulley. It fell now, hurtling down to land exactly where Pepper had been standing, sinking its iron hook into the rope fibers with a noise like tearing gristle. The sailor swore, stared down at the pulley and swore again, looked up at the carpenter, and swore a third time.

Pepper apologized. (The accident had clearly been meant for him, and he was sorry it had given the man such a fright.) The sailor, shamed by the calm of the boy, swallowed his own fright. He pointed away along the quayside to the coaster moored at the other end of the quay. It was no newer than *La Berenice*. In fact it looked to be in a far worse state of repair, rusty and forlorn. "Roux's been transferred. That's his next ship. Would've sailed today, but he's waiting, seemingly. For something. Family troubles. Funeral. Something. Then he'll be off."

"Ah," said Pepper. Well, at least his father planned to be around for the funeral; that was something, Pepper supposed. He turned the big oak pulley over with the toe of his boot. Perhaps he would go up to the hotel, after all, and apologize for being not yet dead.

* * *

Pepper found his father facedown across a table in the backroom bar. Captain Gilbert Roux was so drunk that he could only open his eyes using his finger and thumb. "Who you?" he asked blearily.

"It's Paul," said his son, picking up his father's uniform cap from under the table. "Your son."

"Gone, hazzee? At laasht. Wenza fyooneral?" asked Captain Roux, his cheek smearing spilled ale around the tabletop. Then he let his eyes close again.

"Not today," replied Pepper, and after hovering helplessly for a minute or two, he tugged his father's jacket off the back of the chair.

The bartender was wiping glasses in the front bar as Pepper left. "You're Roux's boy, aren't you?" he asked.

"No. Not me."

Then Pepper walked back down the hill to the harbor. The jacket was far too big for him, but the cap almost fit. (Hat sizes don't vary much with age, only destiny.) So he wore the cap and carried the jacket over his arm when he climbed the gangplank of the coaster *L'Ombrage*.

* * *

14

A new ship. A new crew. How would they ever know?

"Roux," he said, "Captain Roux," and out of the jacket pocket produced the papers to prove it.

The sailor at the head of the gangplank looked him up and down: this skinny, freckled boy, ears bent outward by the rim of a merchant navy cap.

"Set sail," Pepper said. "Now. Right away." Looking over his shoulder toward the hotel on the hill, he only just refrained from saying, *Please. Please hurry!*

There was a pause while the sailor looked around for a second opinion. Then he shouted something toward the bridge, and a head emerged, and a hand too, and someone blew the ship's whistle long and hard.

Pepper drew in his head. The muscles in his calves went rigid, ready to run. The screech of the whistle was so loud that it pained his brain, and it did not stop. They must be summoning the harbormaster! Or the mayor! Or his mother! Saint Constance, or the angel-with-the-fiery-two-edged-sword! The noise of running feet made him spin around.

A man had come tumbling out of the hotel bar and was pelting down the steep road to the harbor, heaving a bag onto his shoulder, shielding his eyes against the bright sun. His ship would be setting sail without him unless he was aboard before the whistle stopped blowing. Pepper watched him, transfixed, certain it was his father. But Gilbert Roux was still so deeply drunk in the back room of the hotel that the Last Trumpet would not have woken him.

The sailor at the head of the gangplank stepped aside with a halfhearted salute to Pepper. "Welcome aboard, Captain," he said.

Well, people see what they expect. Don't they?
Or do they see what they choose?

The panic in Pepper's chest grew worse when he reached the deck. What kind of fool was he to attempt this? Now he would have to steer the ship out of port—rig the masts—plot a course—all those things a sea captain does! How would he ever slot the broad-beamed coaster between the narrow jaws of the harbor's mouth? He would buckle its rusty bow, hole its shabby hull, sink *L'Ombrage*, and cause a shipping hazard for years to come! Absurd ever to think he could pull it off.

But when he reached the bridge, the first officer was already at the helm and too busy maneuvering the ship to notice him. So Pepper went on to the prow. The ship moved at a walking pace toward the green and red poles marking the harbor entrance.

So it passed very close to some boys fishing for eels from the end of the breakwater. Seeing Pepper, one pointed his bamboo cane. An eel dangled from the woollen fishline: a repulsive, puny creature still trying to wriggle out of its fate. "It's you, right?" said the boy. "It is, isn't it? Pepper Roux?"

"Not me," said Pepper, turning away, setting his face toward the horizon. "Not me."

Little by little, the sounds from the shore faded: breaking waves, the carpenters stripping *La Berenice*, the church bells . . . their noises could not leap across the space between shore and ship. Did Death have a longer stride? Would it chase Pepper out to sea? Or could he truly outrun it, throw it off his scent? He had read somewhere that bloodhounds can't follow a scent across water.

He moved to the stern and watched the ship's wake braid itself into a lit fuse in the sun. A flock of seagulls swooped and quarreled and complained overhead: strident, thwarted angels shrieking orange hymns at him. Birds of ill omen. The Hour must be nigh. He watched the sun rise toward midday—a burning magnifying glass trained on a boy of fourteen who had outstayed his welcome.

What would it be, then? A giant wave? The legendary kraken rising, with mile-long tentacles, to drag the ship below? A maelstrom? A sandbar? A reef?

Pepper raised his face flat on to the sky and screamed back at the gulls: "Not me! Not me! Not me!"

Then a hard hand fell on his shoulder.

Pepper turned guiltily— *I'm sorry!*—but it was not his father. Nor the harbormaster, nor even the Angel of Death.

A tall man in rope-soled shoes and sweaty deck clothes looked him in the face, studying each feature as if he were drawing up an inventory. The scar at the corner of the man's cheek twitched. There were flakes of bread crust on his lips, and he licked them clean. If a butcher had been carving the two of them, he would have found twice as much meat on Duchesse, the captain's steward, as on the captain.

"Sun's over the yardarm, sir. All's made ready," said the steward, and led the way to the captain's cabin. He gave the door handle a quick wipe with his neckerchief, then opened it and stood aside. "Everything to hand, sir. Everything aboveboard."

Pepper sat on the bunk, hugging his knees close to his chest without realizing that he was doing it. A chronometer on the wall pointed out the time by chiming the half hour. A chrome speaking tube bent his reflection out of shape. There was a smell like the inside of the wine vat at home.

"It's my birthday," said Pepper.

"Felicitations, Captain," said the steward, which seemed not quite to cover the disastrousness of the situation. Then he poured a full glass of something brown and presented it to Pepper on a little round tray. When Pepper did not reach for it, Duchesse folded the boy's small ice-cold hands around the glass and held them there until the brown liquor stopped slopping over the sides. "*Santé*, Captain. Happy birthday."

The drink scorched his throat. Perhaps it was poison. Pepper rested his head on the pillow and counted to a hundred. Maybe the Angel of Death went about in rope-soled shoes and a sweaty neckerchief.

Outside, there was a commotion, and the ancient engine slowed again. A boat thudded lightly against the hull, and there was shouting on deck. Duchesse cocked his head to listen. Pepper covered his ears and shut his eyes, all too sure of who was being hauled aboard by the crew. His father must have rowed out to the ship and caught it after all.

"Roche," said Duchesse, loosing the word like spittle. Then he gave a short laugh. "He'll soon wish he'd missed *this* sailing, eh, sir?"

Squinting out of the porthole, Pepper could see an empty rowboat being hauled aboard by its mooring rope, banging up against the ship's side. The latecomer was offering violence to anyone who came near him. The crash of his boots came closer and closer . . . but mercifully passed by the captain's cabin.

"Never fear, dear heart," said the steward soothingly. "Leave it to the Duchess. I will endeavor to keep the pig from troubling you."

As the cabin door closed softly behind Duchesse, the sunlight falling between the door's wooden slats sliced the room into strips of light and dark. Pepper shut his eyes.

When he opened them again, the room was gray with evening. He looked out of the porthole and saw a navy sky swagged with vast gray wings of cloud.

From horizon to horizon, the sea seemed to be netted over—like a strawberry bed—with angels. How had he ever hoped to escape? Aunt Mireille's voice rang in his ears:

> *"No escaping, boy. As the Good Book says, you can try taking the wings of the morning, and dwelling in the uttermost parts of the sea: The Lord will still hunt you down and grab ahold of you."*

What would become of *L'Ombrage,* then, and its crew? Would the saints consult their pocket watches, tut-tut, and put things back on schedule? Would they plunge the entire ship to the ocean floor to ensure that Pepper met his end on time? That wasn't fair. That wasn't fair to the crew at all!

Stumbling to the door, Pepper tugged it open and ran. Best to get it over and done with. Best to leap the ship's rail like Jonah and spare his men! He would leap outward—far and far—from the ship, and the oily black of the sea would hide all noise, all panic, all second thoughts and third and fourth thoughts too. . . .

In the dark he tripped over a pair of legs sticking out from under a lifeboat. A figure pulled itself out into the open and rolled across him, hunchbacked with muscle and rolls of fat, to press its forehead against Pepper's, supported by hands on either side of Pepper's head. "Look where you're going, you ?#@*&," said a mouth reeking of rum and garlic before it bit him in the ear. "Come dark, this here's *my* ship. Got that? Shall I teach yuh?"

Captain Pepper rolled sideways and scuttled—on hands and knees, then hands and feet, then at full tilt—*"Sorry! Sorry! Sorry!"*—back to his cabin, where he crawled under his bunk and lay wide-eyed with terror. His little heart was ready to burst with it—especially when the chronometer began to chime—on and on and on. Eight bells. *Midnight.* The last chime died away.

What? Still alive?

Was the clock in Heaven's parlor running slow? Had his mother misremembered the date fourteen years earlier? Had Saint Constance of the Perfect Diction put in an elegant word for him with the Angel of Death?

Or had Pepper truly stepped sideways into his father's life and out of his own?

TWO

SKELETON MAN

No ship's crew minds if they see nothing of their captain. To a crew, captains mean only orders, unwelcome amounts of work, the finding of faults. The crew of *L'Ombrage* did not complain at all when their new captain chose to stay in his cabin. They simply hoped their luck would hold. Some people can be wished invisible.

When Pepper woke next morning in his father's bunk, he looked around the cabin and counted seven glasses of rum. One stood on the table, one on either side of the washbowl, another on the corner of the bunk, one on the clothes chest, one beside the door, and one on the chart desk. The dark liquid inside

23

rocked in time to the steady dipping of the ship. They had just been poured by his steward, who stood now in the doorway, surveying the room to spot any task he had overlooked. Duchesse had ironed Pepper's clothing, polished his shoes, washed his underpants and supplied a spare pair, laid out a breakfast of sardines and soda bread, filled the ewer with hot water, altered the date on the brass calendar, and wound the brass chronometer. And he had filled the seven glasses of rum, which, in his experience, it took for an alcoholic captain to rise, dress, and confront the new day. Whatever had made the grotesque scar below Duchesse's left eye seemed to have spared his sight, for his small, gleaming eyes missed nothing, skirted over nothing—except perhaps the captain himself.

"Fine morning, Captain," he said, as if he had somehow managed to arrange that too. Then he pushed bare feet back into his rope-soled shoes, smoothed the pleats of the kilt he was now wearing, and closed the cabin door behind him.

The problem of actually sailing the ship still worried Pepper, but luckily the first officer did all that for him.

First Officer Berceau was happy with the arrangement. He had heard tell of Roux's drinking and had sailed with drunken captains before. They would wrench the helm out of his hands so as to go looking for mermaids, or draw wriggly lines on his clean chart and tear holes in it. They would write down sightings of nonexistent islands in the ship's log in drunken, looping letters. No, it suited Berceau perfectly if the Old Man drank himself insensible in his cabin and never appeared on the bridge at all.

"The Old Man." Several times those words drifted in through the louvered door of Pepper's cabin to bewilder him. At first he imagined the men were being sarcastic, but he soon realized that "Old Man" was simply naval slang for "captain." And so long as this particular "Old Man" did not come out of his cabin and try to command the ship, they would be relaxed, happy . . . and bone idle.

The crew used lots of interesting words and phrases Pepper had never come across before; words so much more expressive than the language spoken at home. He sometimes asked Duchesse to translate, so that he could master the words himself, but Duchesse declined. "Officers operate a different philology from crew," he said with a sniff, and straightened the toga he was wearing that day with the haughty dignity of a Roman senator.

Dust settled on the seven poured glasses of rum, and the Duchess (who dusted everything else) let it lie. What the Old Man did in the privacy of his cabin was no business of anyone but his and his steward's. Duchesse never mentioned to his comrades that this particular Old Man was teetotal. He did not mention the prayers he found tucked inside the captain's laundry, but left them in a neat pile for Pepper to pocket again. Nor did he reveal that the captain seemed to own only one pair of underpants and a jacket that did not fit him.

In fact, on the third morning, a new, well-fitting jacket swung and swayed on the back of the cabin door, and onto it had been sewn all the braids and ribbons from the old one. So Pepper was better able to go up on deck, down to the boiler room, and up and down the companionways. Hands clasped behind his back, Captain "Pepper" Roux surveyed his vessel: looked up at the mast tops, down into the hold, and out to sea at the weather.

L'Ombrage seemed to be carrying a cargo of scrap iron. Pepper wondered: Were the English too rich or too poor to have any scrap iron of their own, so that they had to send all the way to France for it? And why did it say on his father's papers that *L'Ombrage* was carrying pianos and fine porcelain?

Pepper was busy wondering this when he stepped in a puddle of playing cards and tore one of them in half. He had walked into the middle of a card game, and four squatting sailors looked up at him, annoyed. Pepper saw nothing of them, only the symbol on the torn playing card—the ace of spades: unluckiest card in the pack. It hit him quite as hard as a full-size shovel. With a yelp, he turned and ran for his cabin.

He found the Duchess—dressed today in a sarong—grating Parmesan cheese over a plate of scrambled eggs.

"Your favorite, Captain," said the Duchess tenderly.

And it was true! Pepper had seen his mother serve scrambled eggs to his father on every shore leave with much the same anxious tenderness: *Your favorite, dear.*

"How do you know?" Pepper said, before he could help himself.

The Duchess smiled one of the slow smiles that puckered his scar into the shape of a rosette. "After sailing together all these years, sir? Remiss of me not to know your little weaknesses."

Not an entirely *new crew, then.*

Pepper sat down sharply and, all the while he ate, waited in terror for the Duchess to say more. But the steward only continued his round of chores, changing the linen on the bunk, fixing a troublesome squeak in the boards. On hands and knees he chased that mousy squeak, cornering it beside the locker and killing it with a hammer. The noise made Pepper blink at last and realize that his eyeballs were dry from staring at the dirt-blackened soles of Duchesse's enormous bare feet. As Pepper laid down his knife and fork, the Duchess stood up—the low deckhead made him stoop—thrust his feet back into his espadrilles, and picked up Pepper's dirty dishes.

"Are there any more . . . old comrades of ours aboard?" asked Pepper in a high, breathy whisper.

"Just me, sir."

And never again did Duchesse refer to the twenty years he had spent as steward to Captain Gilbert Roux.

Pepper did not know enough of the world to think the Duchess unusual. But he began to pick up from the crew that his steward was in some way . . . remarkable. The clothes he wore on board had been collected during a lifetime's voyages to exotic parts. The men smiled affectionately whenever they saw him—stepped aside as he swaggered along the ship, swaying his broad hips, swishing grass skirts, or sporting a sombrero. As well as fetching Pepper his dinner and his laundry, he brought messages from the first officer. "First sends his compliments, sir, and wonders if the ship would look prettier with a navigation lamp or two lit."

Others of the sailors got into arguments or card games, but the Duchess never quarreled or neglected his duties. Tenderly he waited on the captain, so that the captain need never stir. He shouted orders into the shiny speaking tube—"Captain says to blow through the boiler tubes"—leaving Pepper feeling as thrilled as if he really had been the one to give the order. He also brought Pepper the ship's log, politely pointing out "how white the pages looked" without the captain's daily entry. "I could dictate, sir, if the words won't come to mind."

Pepper swallowed hard. His father, though new to *L'Ombrage,* had already made several entries in its battered log, using wild, looping copperplate handwriting, and ink. Pepper knew he could never imitate such fancy writing, never having used a fountain pen.

"If Captain has *hurt his writing hand,* perhaps he should *use his left* when making his entries in the log," observed Duchesse, replacing Pepper's supper plate with the open leather-bound book.

"And a pencil?" asked Pepper.

"And a pencil, sir."

So Pepper began to feel more at ease with his steward—not enough to confess his dreadful secret, of course, but he did pluck up the courage to mention his biggest worry—the one about a giant kraken rising from the ocean bed and eating the ship.

The Duchess considered this for a moment, then said, "I don't believe there is a single kraken left living between Marseille and Gravesend. Far too much traffic, *chéri.*"

Pepper wanted to believe him.

Old habits die hard, though, and next day, Pepper felt the need to climb up high and scan the four horizons: for kraken, tidal waves, or maelstroms, for fiery chariots or Saint Constance sculling toward him in a rowboat. So he climbed the mast, nimble, sure-footed, up to the crosstrees, where he perched beside the masthead light, looking out to sea. The air up there smelled of salt and the black smoke from the funnel. He could see right down the funnel and, around it, see the whole petal-shaped deck scribbled through with a web of stay ropes. He could see the horizon and the hammered-metal sea, and it soothed him. He could see his crew standing openmouthed, gazing up at him so far below. "I can see you *all*!" he called down, in a sudden burst of affection. *"Every one of you!"*

He would do this every day, yes! He could hardly explain to his men how, by running away to sea, he had put all their lives at risk. But if, from up here, he were to spot sea monsters or freak waves in the offing, he could at least shout down, "Abandon ship!" Also, he was giving Fate the chance (if it wanted) to knock him off the crosstrees and kill him, without dooming the whole crew. That seemed only fair, and Pepper was a stickler for fairness.

No sooner did his feet touch the deck than the

31

Duchess hurried him back to the captain's cabin, scolding him for "making the heart jump clear out of me, you naughty man!"

"I was just checking we were safe," said Pepper.

"Safe? Safe?" roared the Duchess, swigging down one of the seven glasses of dusty rum. "God's in his girdle, of course we're bloody safe!"

But the Duchess was forgetting Roche.

Roche was a pear-shaped man, hunchbacked with rolls of fat and muscle, who delighted in making the younger members of the crew do any duty he was given to do himself. In port, he would lay his own pay packet on the table and tell the boys, "Yours—if you can buy me enough drink to make me pass out." In this way he never had to buy himself a drink. Or lose his wages. For drink never made Roche pass out. It only made him foulmouthed, violent, and clumsy. It made him lurch about the ship, his flat feet splayed, cannoning into rails and bulwarks, kicking and cursing them for getting in his way.

Any ship at night was Roche's happy hunting ground. He slept naked on deck, glistening like a side

of bacon, or prowled the vessel, unscrewing brass fit-
ments that he sold to chandleries ashore. The fact that
L'Ombrage seemed already to have been stripped of all
her valuable fittings was the first thing to vex him.
Then Roche discovered, too late, the name of her captain. And the hatred that name aroused in him made
him more dangerous than any kraken.

The idea began to haunt Pepper that his father had
somehow, somewhere, come aboard the ship. Every
night he dreamed that Gilbert Roux was rattling at the
door, lurking in the hold, prowling the decks, wanting
his life back. Even awake, he imagined he could hear
his father searching the ship, and would lie in pools of
his own sweat, wondered if stealing a vessel from its
captain was still punishable by hanging.

If he had been onshore, he would have confessed all
to the village priest. The worst things about going to
confession with Father Ignatius every other day had
been trying to think of something to confess; the look
of intense boredom on the priest's face when Pepper
arrived; the noise of yawning from the other com-
partment of the confessional box. How much more

interesting Pepper could have made the poor man's tedious job now, with these ghastly sins of his. Defying his parents and all the saints. Lying. Theft. Maybe even piracy!

"I know you!"

The voice came so readily through the door slats that it might as well have been in the same room. Pepper gripped the side of his bunk and stared at the door.

"If I'd knowed it was you, I'd of never . . ." The voice was drunken, the mouth pressed so close to the door that Pepper could hear the wetness of sloppy lips. It did not *sound* like his father's voice, but who else . . . ? "Famous, *you* are," jeered the voice. "Everyone knows what *you* are."

What? A boy who couldn't sail a ship? A boy too scared to do as he is told and die? A boy pretending to be someone else? But a good boy, basically? A harmless boy? He had tried, hadn't he? To remember all the *thou shalt*s and *thou shalt not*s in the Ten Commandments? To memorize all the psalms, and all the *begat*s and *begotten*s of the Old Testament?

"Forgive me, Father, for I have sinned," whispered the boy in the bunk, as he had each day at confession.

34

But this time, the silhouette on the other side of the grille was not a priest offering forgiveness.

"Climbing the mast to spy on us! Climbing up there to lord it over us with your *'I can see you.'* Well, I know what you are, Roux! I can see *you*—scum that you are!" A cold sweat steeped Pepper from head to foot as the final words were formed and came slobbering through the door: *"You're the Skeleton Man!"*

Pepper did not sleep for the rest of the night. Coiled up under his bunk, he wept salt tears and felt the caress of kraken tentacles up and down his flesh.

Next day, *L'Ombrage* passed Finisterre and headed into grayer waters. By evening, she had left behind all sight of land. There was a knock at the cabin door.

"Bill of lading for the first officer, dear heart?" said the Duchess. Instead of saluting, he pressed his palms together and bowed, as befitted the Japanese kimono he was wearing.

"Bill who?"

"Paperwork. Listing the cargo, dear heart? It is customary." Duchesse looked at him, head on one side, and winked.

"Give me a minute."

Pepper closed the door, biting his lip. He had no idea what a bill of lading looked like, or even how it was spelled. In his weariness he could make no sense of the documents on the cabin desk. He could find nothing mentioning scrap iron. Pianos and porcelain, yes, but nothing about scrap iron, nothing about scrap iron, nothing about forgiveness or scrap iron. He even scrabbled up the blotting paper off the blotter, in his panic.

Underneath lay a folded sheet of paper bearing the name of the owners: Maritime Sud & Cie. The bill of lading, surely!

No. Nothing about scrap iron. Only a map position—45° 20' N, 6° 54' W—oh, and a pencil sketch alongside, obviously drawn by someone bored and doodling.

It was the sketch of a skull.

Pepper's eyes rolled upward and his lids fluttered. He pitched forward and cracked his head on the desk. The last thing he heard was the crackle of his ears as they escaped the rim of his naval cap.

A skeleton climbed up out of Aunty Mireille's teacup, then crawled between her plate and the toast rack to admire its

reflection in the saltcellar. Pepper tried to spear it with his
fork but missed, and it clambered on toward him across
the breakfast table, laughing as it came. . . .

A hand momentarily stroked the back of his head and
stirred him back to consciousness.

"A big mistake, to use letterhead paper," said the
Duchess, tugging the sheet out of Pepper's fist. He
memorized the figures—45° 20' N, 6° 54' W—then
set it alight with a match. "Especially with the added
sketch, silly boys. Tell them not to do it again, *chéri,*
when you collect your bonus." He reached out a finger, lifted Pepper's bangs, and winced at the size of the
bump on his forehead.

"You don't understand, Duchesse! It's a sign! That's
where! That's where it's going to happen!"

Duchesse studied the captain's pinched, weary,
tearstained face for a long time. "Mmm. But then it
won't be our first, will it, dear heart?" he said, leaning
on the words as if they were brass tacks. "You and I are
old hands at this game. Like undertakers, we deal in
coffins. . . . It's a bit late for us to try to change the way
things work *in the coffin trade.*"

And Pepper took the hint and fell silent. Because

either he was Paul Roux, an ignorant boy pretending to be his father, or he *was* Captain Gilbert Roux, drink-sodden Old Man of *L'Ombrage* and several other ill-fated ships. Pepper was going to die, at 45° 20' N, 6° 54' W, but then—as Duchesse said—it was a bit late to try to change Fate.

Pepper sat for so long—frozen with fear, head throbbing—that the sun passed overhead and *L'Ombrage* chugged into the Bay of Biscay. The speaking tube squealed once, but he ignored it. He heard—briefly— the hatch cover outside being raised by winch and cable. Strange. (Perhaps England was very close now— how would he know?) The Duchess came with a tray of supper, but Pepper did not open the door to him. "I'm not hungry. Go away."

It was a shame. He had loved the sea—every indigo smell of it, every dolphin, every kicking wave, every whooping cheer that broke from the ship's whistle. He loved Duchesse's scrambled eggs, and the gold braid on his captain's jacket, and sliding the cap onto his head, folding his ears forward to keep it high on his brow. A shame for it all to end. But tonight he would—he really must—search the ship until he found his father, wherever he was lurking, and hand back the cap, the papers, the ship's log: name and rank. Say sorry. Gilbert Roux (Captain) might flog him or hang him from the yardarm for piracy, but it could not be helped. Pepper had not been to confession for a week, so if he died now, unpunished, he would certainly go to Hell and be punished forevermore, and that would be worse.

Aunty Mireille had taught him lots about Hell.

That night, moonlight puddled and curded on the decks, turning them white. Pepper half expected to skid as he scoured the ship for Gilbert Roux. He looked in the paint store and under the lifeboat covers. The hatch of the hold had indeed been lifted slightly—as if to keep the scrap iron from suffocating—but nothing moved down there. In fact all he found, after ten minutes' searching . . . was Roche sitting naked astride the ship's rail.

"Be very careful, Mr. Roche," said Pepper, worried that the man might slip into the sea.

Roche's head snapped up, and the moonlight turned his face ghost white.

"What are you doing?" asked Pepper, knowing that it

is polite to express an interest in other people's work.

Roche opened his left hand, and Pepper went closer, thinking he was being shown something. It seemed to be one of those brackets used to hang up the fire buckets. Moving close also filled his nose with a familiar smell: one he had not smelled since it had sunk its teeth in his ear. Fate smelled of garlic and rum, thought Pepper, as Roche swung his leg inboard, shifted the metal bracket into his right fist, and slashed at him with its hook.

"Skeleton Man."

Pepper ran, but Roche was so close behind that the hook hit him repeatedly on the shoulders, then snagged in the half belt of his jacket and was pulled out of Roche's fist. Pepper collided with the various sand-filled fire buckets that Roche had lifted down so as to steal the brackets. Sand hissed across the deck. There was nowhere to hide. Even his thoughts could not catch their breath.

If I say . . . the darkness shall cover me. . . . Yea, the darkness is no darkness. . . .

"Mama! Aunty Mireille!" The half belt came unstitched: The hook, still embedded in its fabric, banged into the back of Pepper's legs as he ran. "Saint

Constance! Father Michel! Mama! Holy Mary!" But maybe the saints and angels locked up house at night and shut their shutters, as Mama had always done. "Roche! Stop! I'm the captain! Don't!"

He almost tripped over the partly raised hatch cover: The hold gaped below him like the mouth of Hell, and the smell of Roche was in every breath that he gulped down. Colliding with the foot of the funnel, Pepper began to climb—if he could just get up high!—but feeling for handholds, he soon met only with hot metal, and dropped back down, fully expecting to land in Roche's arms.

His fall to the deck knocked the wind out of him. Nothing softened his landing. Nothing. Nothing and no one.

Looking back the way he had come, Pepper imagined the momentary flicker of an angel's white, lacy robe. But of Roche there was not a sign. Gasping and reeling, he fled to his cabin and spent the rest of the night on his callused knees, burned palms pressed together, apologizing to everyone in Heaven that he could think of for the sin of being alive.

* * *

He supposed the knock at the door was Duchesse bringing his breakfast, but it was the first officer. Pepper (remembering the lost bill of lading) hastily shut the door in his face. What to do? Berceau knocked again, louder and more urgently. Pepper opened the door.

"Accident on deck, sir," said Berceau. "Roche has . . . taken a tumble."

Apparently, Roche had lost his footing during one of his nightly prowls, skidded on some spilled sand, and fallen twenty feet into the open hold, landing on a length of rusty metal fencing. His face had the agonized, waxy whiteness of the saints in the church at home.

So this was what a fall looked like: neither quick nor clean.

Pepper went down on his knees in the cluttered hold. "Don't worry, Roche. Lie still, Roche. Soon get you out, Roche," said Captain Pepper Roux.

Roche opened a red-rimmed mouth, but no words came out. He looked up at the square of sky above them, and seagull shapes drifted across his vacant eyes. The crew had thrown a blanket over him, but a line of sharp points still stuck up through the cloth, like the bony spine on a mackerel. Rummaging in his jacket pocket, Pepper brought out a prayer, penned in his aunt's purple ink on lilac notepaper—a prayer to Saint Constance.

> *Kindly pray for us sinners now and at the hour of our death.*
>
> *Your obedient servant,*
Mireille Lepont (Miss)

It was hard to know where to put it on a naked man, so Pepper tucked it into Roche's armpit, murmuring an apology.

For surely the fall had been meant for Pepper? Surely the seagulls had gathered over the site of a death days overdue? The hold had yawned for Pepper but accidentally swallowed Roche.

The man impaled on the scrap iron turned his eyes on Pepper, reached out a trembling hand, and caught him by the throat. The hand was very cold, and powerless to grip. Taking it in his own, Pepper began to recite the last rites, tugging each icy finger in turn, just as his aunty had done for him when he was little.

But before the end, the hand slackened and the eyes turned upward into the skull. Roche had mopped up death like a lump of bread mopping a greasy plate.

THREE
PROTESTER

The business of the last rites vastly impressed the crew of *L'Ombrage*, gathered around the brink of the hold. For the first time, they looked at their Old Man with startled respect. They were even more impressed when Captain Roux proved to know the funeral service by heart . . . though no one offered to pry Roche off the rusty metalwork, so Pepper had to stop short of the bit about committing him "to the sea in the sure and certain hope of salvation."

"Later," said Berceau.

Nobody dressed up for the service either, except the Duchess, who put on red satin as a mark of disrespect.

"Amen," said Pepper at the end of the Lord's Prayer.

"Good riddance," said the crew—which was not a response Pepper had ever heard before but which he presumed was a special seagoing expression of farewell. His efforts gave Pepper no joy: Couched on his scrap-metal bed, Roche did not look to be any more at peace because of all those words.

Later that day, with Roche's body still lying in the hold, Duchesse came and broke the bad news. "Married man," he said.

"No I'm not!" exclaimed Pepper, and sat back in his captain's chair so sharply that it almost toppled over.

"Roche, dear heart," said the Duchess patiently. "Roche was a married man. The customary letter is required. To the widow."

And here, for the first time, was a duty no one else was willing to do for Captain Pepper.

"Not my province," said the Duchess.

"Not me," said the second mate.

"Not me," said Berceau, spotting the bill of lading on the floor and smoothing it out against his thigh. *Pianos and porcelain,* it read.

"Doesn't he have . . . didn't he have a best friend? Someone who's known him for a long time?" Pepper begged them.

But Roche had no friends. So Captain Pepper was obliged to sit at his desk with a blank sheet of paper in front of him and a pencil in his hand. He wrote the name of the ship in one corner. He wrote the address of the widow in the other. He wrote: *I am very sorry to say. . . .*

Then he sent for the crew.

They all squeezed into his cabin, elbow to elbow, knees slightly bent because of the low deckhead. What did they know about Mr. Roche? asked Pepper.

"He was a pig," said Annecy.

"Used to bet the deck boys he could knock them down with one punch," said Gombert. "Broke their faces. Took their money."

"Beat his wife," said Bougon. "Used to boast about it."

"Don't know how she lives. He spent all his money on whores; never sent a penny home."

"He sold the pans out of the galley," said the cook bitterly.

"Heard he killed a man once, in Nantes."

47

Pepper sighed. "There's good in everyone," he suggested hopefully. "My priest says . . ."

"He was good with his fists," said Annecy.

"Perhaps you could share with us some of your own impressions of the man, sir," suggested the Duchess, fretful at having the captain's private sanctum cluttered up with people.

Pepper thought hard. "He wanted to kill me."

The assembled crew nodded thoughtfully. "He was a rare pig, that one," said Annecy.

"Amen," said the others, and squeezed out of the door again.

Pepper stared at the blank paper. A dozen times he wrote the address and began:

I am awfuly sorry . . .

I am paned to tell you . . .

I hope you wont . . .

I wish I did not have to in form you . . .

He imagined the woman—Mme. Yvette Roche—opening and reading his letter. In his imagination, she took on the face of his own mother: the shoulders folding forward, the head sinking into grief.

L'Ombrage

Apartment 19
27 rue Méjeunet
Aigues Mortes

Dear Madame Roche,
    I am very sorry in deed to tell you the sad
news, but your poor husbund Monsieur Roche is
dead. I did not no him very well, but I expect you
did. I am sure he is happy with the saints.
                    Your obediant servent . . .

Pepper snatched up the letter and crammed it into his pocket. On the whole, he thought she would much rather not know at all. That way, she could go on hoping all was not lost, even when it was.

"How will she manage without the money?" he asked. But the Duchess simply went on grating nutmeg over a bowl of custard. "I say we should . . . I mean, could we . . . What say we don't tell the owners about Roche being dead? That way they won't stop his wages—not till the end of the trip, anyway."

The Duchess did look up, then, and Pepper assumed nutmegs must be like onions, for there were tears in the steward's eyes. "I think that would be a very great kindness to his wife, *mon brave*."

The next thought made Pepper's gorge heave, but one of his duties as captain was surely to help a dead crew member find eternal rest. "I expect you could make him a nice shroud, Duchesse, if I could just get him off the . . . get him up out . . . get him into the sea."

For the first time since they had met, the steward was completely at a loss. "Well, he can go down with the ship, can't he?" he said, hurrying to the door, sickened by the horrific notion of Pepper wrestling with a corpse. Outside, Duchesse recovered his calm, smoothed his red satin, and patted his hair into place. Then he caught hold of the nearest crew member by the shirt, dragged him close, and laid a finger to his lips. Never again did the crew mention the name of Roche or the small matter of his death.

"Who'd miss a pig like that?" observed Annecy.

Sometimes a shipping company can make more money from losing a ship than from keeping it. After all, ships are forever sinking, so they are always insured. A ship with a cargo of pianos and porcelain is insured for far more than some rusty, dilapidated hulk carrying scrap iron. And once that ship is sunk and on the seabed, who is to say what cargo she was carrying? She will keep her secret as well as a dead man in his coffin. Maybe that is why such hulks are called "coffin ships."

At position 45° 20' N, 6° 54' W, with a dirty sea running and *L'Ombrage* sitting over 2,600 fathoms of water, the engineer deliberately opened her sea cocks. Sip by sip, she began to swallow the sea. Only the engineer, Berceau, and Gilbert Roux were being paid by the owners to sink her. The Duchess was in on it, of course. But the rest of the crew were told *L'Ombrage* had sprung a leak and were as scared as if *L'Ombrage* had hit an iceberg or been attacked by the kraken.

"Time to go," said the captain's steward to the captain.

"Why?"

Duchesse looked exasperated. With the ship's claxon blaring and the air as full of filthy language as spray, even the old-style, drunken Captain Roux might have grasped that the ship was sinking. "Time to go," said the Duchess again. He was dressed once more in trousers and oiled jersey, and had hacked his hair short with a pair of scissors.

"No. It's all right. I'll stay," said Pepper. He had read enough books, after all, and he knew the rules. It was a shame: Drowning had come very low down his list of favored deaths—somewhere between suffocating and the guillotine. But he knew the rules: A good captain goes down with his ship.

The scar on Duchesse's cheek puckered. "That really isn't required."

"Oh, I think it is," said Pepper. "You see . . . I shouldn't be here."

"Never a truer word, *petite framboise*," said Duchesse as the ship groaned and began to list. "Don't forget the log."

Pepper fetched the leather-bound log and gave it into his steward's hands. "There. I haven't messed it up too much." There was shouting outside, as those abandoning ship struggled with a faulty boat winch. "I'm a Jonah," said Pepper, and took one step back. "I'm the one it's after, you see." Then he stood, chin up, hands behind his back, waiting for the water to fill the cabin like a fish tank.

Duchesse's eyebrows shot up, and after a second, a kind of laugh erupted from his nose. "Is this the kraken we're talking about here?"

"You don't understand."

Duchesse looked over his shoulder. He did not understand, no. But there was a very particular timing to these operations; they had not a second to lose. "The owners don't want this. . . . This is insane, boy. He must've told you! He must've told you when he sent you in his place?"

"'If I dwell in the uttermost parts of the sea,'" said Pepper unhelpfully, and bent forward the tips of his ears before sliding on his naval cap.

"Sir's scared to get into the lifeboat! Is that it? I could blindfold sir! Like a horse!"

But Pepper had had plenty of time to think up an answer to every temptation. The saints had made it abundantly clear what they thought of his ducking and diving; they had even posted him a note under his blotter. "If I get into that boat, it won't reach land. I told you. I'm a Jonah. The angels are after me."

Duchesse's color deepened with his dismay. The Bay of Biscay had shrouded *L'Ombrage* in spray, and large waves were breaking over the starboard bow, making her wallow. Running to the speaking tube, he bawled into it, "Keep her head into the wind, you ?#@*&s!" Then he hurried outside to help free the winch of the lifeboat.

The engineer was the last into the boat, received into the upstretched hands of the men below, like a shrimp into an anemone. Though he had stopped the engine before leaving, the ship was still noisy with banging doors, falling crates, crashing spray, creaking joints. It was uncomfortably wet and treacherous on deck, too, now that the ship was listing and side-on to the swell. Even so, Captain Pepper decided not to stay in his cabin, but to crawl and stagger for'ard to the hold, where he sat down on its rim.

He understood now why the hatch had been opened—so that the water could enter top as well as bottom, and take the ship swiftly to the seabed. It would not do for the crew of some passing boat to see her in difficulties, board her, and discover the sea cocks open. Oh, it was not that Pepper had failed to grasp the whole idea of coffin ships and insurance scams—he had always been quick on the uptake. It was Duchesse who did not understand. *L'Ombrage*, on her shabby, risky, dishonest final voyage, had strayed accidentally into the path of something much more dangerous: a boyhunt. Angels and saints were even now harpooning the ocean with forked lightning, shaking the tarpaulin waves, loosing windy howls, and snorting up the spray for scent of a missing boy, a boy *overdue*. Aunt Mireille had always said that unpunctuality is the height of bad manners, and Pepper had purposely tried to be late for his death. He really must not keep Saint Constance waiting any longer.

"We commit our bodies to the sea, in the sure and certain hope," he remarked to Roche, whose body was submerged now under a fathom of water and beckoning to Pepper with both bare arms. "Don't we?" The listing ship groaned. Down below, empty clothes hangers in Duchesse's locker all fell down at the same moment, with a noise like a skeleton gone mad.

"Bless me, Father, for I think I might have sinned," said Pepper, but there were no fathers—the good kind or the bad—aboard the dying *Ombrage*. The hatch cover shifted and the cable bearing its weight slipped on its drum with a terrible screaming noise. The dead Roche beckoned. . . .

"Sun's over the yardarm, Captain," said a voice

behind Pepper. "Everything to hand, sir. Everything aboveboard. I think a drink might be in order."

Duchesse helped Pepper to his feet and returned him to the captain's cabin, where he pointed out six dusty glasses of rum. Because of the ship's list, each of them stood aslope now, the rum inside just starting to lap out onto the floor. Duchesse abhorred waste. When Pepper said he did not drink, Duchesse said, "There's always a first time, *chéri*. And the last time's as good a time as any for the first time." *One*.

When Pepper said he was shivering not from fright but from cold, Duchesse said, "The rum will warm you up." *Two*.

When Pepper admitted he was shivering from fright, Duchesse said, "Rum's not called 'Dutch courage' for nothing." *Three*.

"That's gin, isn't it?" said Pepper, whose family library had taught him an odd assortment of facts.

"Here's to a broad general knowledge," said Duchesse. "A wonderful thing." And they shared the fourth glass. The drink scorched Pepper's throat like poison, but Duchesse folded the boy's small, ice-cold hands around each glass and held them there until the brown liquid stopped slopping. "*Santé*, Captain."

"You should have gotten off with the others! Why didn't you get off? Why didn't you?"

The Duchess sat back comfortably in his chair. "Life hasn't suited me lately," he said, as if life were a fashion trend and his hips too broad to carry it off.

When Pepper said that he was going to be sick, Duchesse insisted a glass of rum would settle his stomach. *Five.*

The sixth glass no one drank, because it—or was it the ship?—had tilted too far, and trickled the contents onto the floor. Pepper rested his head on the pillow and began to count. By the time he reached fourteen . . .

. . . he was deeply unconscious.

When Pepper woke the next day—or was it the week after?—he knew, from the chugging of engines, that he was still on board ship. But he also knew this ship must be bound for Hell. Scarlet-and-green demons were squatting around all four edges of the ceiling. Their claws gripping tight to stacked plywood crates, they squawked and tutted, peering down at him from behind huge beaks. Aunty Mireille had taught Pepper lots about demons and how they loved to rend and tear the souls of the damned, but she had not mentioned the beaks. These were what she must have meant by "birds of ill omen."

There were demons inside his head, too, tearing at his brain, and he felt very, very sick. Every time he closed his eyes, he pictured *L'Ombrage* on her slow plunge through transparent darkness and cold toward the bottom of the sea. Was he still aboard her and breathing water? He wondered if information was allowed in Hell, because more than anything, Pepper wanted to know whether Duchesse and the rest of the crew had been saved. The demons clacked their beaks and fluttered, but they wouldn't answer his questions.

While he had lain there unconscious, every piece of braid had been laboriously picked off his uniform jacket—who by?—leaving him drab. That was fair, he supposed. It probably said something in the Bible about gold braid: *Vanity of vanities, all braid is vanity, saith the preacher.* Naturally, ranks were not allowed in the underworld, he quite understood that. No rank, no escape, no saying sorry. But it was strange to find Aunty's prayers still in his pocket . . . along with a slender roll of banknotes that had not been there before.

Demon droppings fell like hail as the door opened and a Malay sailor brought in a bowl of rice and a cup of water.

"May I ask questions?" asked Pepper.

But the Malay only bowed and smiled, set the food down, and bowed again before leaving, no more able to understand the French language than he could the squawks of the parakeets tethered to the cargo crates.

When Pepper went up on deck (the door of the cell was not locked, but two days passed before he thought to try it), a sight rose out of the sea that was very like the Gates of Heaven, shimmering. Perhaps, after all, the angels had caught him in their nets and were drawing him home according to plan.

But the vision proved to be only the city of Marseille, gilded yellow by its usual pall of pollution. After the ship docked, the crew presented Pepper with a gift of small macaroons and an umbrella, gesturing toward the shore, smiling and bowing. Pepper descended the gangplank.

* * *

All Pepper lacked now was a reason to set one foot in front of the other. For what use is a sea captain without a ship—or a crew—or a steward with an array of jolly costumes? Anyway, he did not want to be Captain Gilbert Roux, defrauder of insurance companies, drink-sodden sinker of ships. There must have been better lives to hide inside.

It was a bright, sunny day, but as he walked down the street, he felt water drops on his face and put up his new umbrella. The water was coming from fire hoses at the end of the street. The local fire brigade was hosing down a group of protesters gathered in front of the town hall. The water pressure was low, so the demonstrators were not being knocked off their feet so much as gently doused, like potted plants watered from a high window. They milled around—men, women, and students—carrying placards and chanting doggedly up at the closed windows of the town hall. They had the look of clerks or shop assistants, in grays and browns. But their faces were bright with excitement and outrage, as if the protest had livened up a tedious week. Even the hoses were only making them gasp and giggle.

Pepper couldn't make out what they were chanting.

He went closer to read the words painted on their soggy placards:

REPEAL CLAUSE FIVE OF THE HONGRIOT-PLEUVIEZ AMENDMENT! REPEAL IT NOW!

Pepper gave his umbrella to a woman who had curled her hair that morning and wanted to keep it nice. The demonstrators closed around him, like schooling fish, and he found himself part of the protest, given a placard to hold:

DOWN WITH THE HONGRIOT-PLEUVIEZ AMENDMENT (CLAUSE 5)!

"Excuse me . . . I don't quite know what the—" he began, but the chanting scribbled out his words.

The women had started up a simpler chant: *"Hear what we say! Repeal the HPA!"*

In his drab, braidless jacket, Pepper was a tadpole in a pool of other tadpoles. Water ran down his neck, his shoes squelched, but apart from that, it was a good feeling. The dockside clock struck noon, and the fire brigade stopped for lunch.

So the demonstrators went to buy their lunches from the grocery store on the corner. Rather than stand alone in a puddle outside the town hall in a strange town, Pepper tagged along. The grocery store was closed. The students of philosophy accepted this philosophically, with a shrug, but the clerks were in a reckless mood and decided they would go up to the grand department store at the top of the hill and buy sausage from the delicatessen there. It would be an outrageous extravagance, but demonstrating had made them all feel slightly bigger, bolder, more deserving than on a normal working day. Hungrier, too.

Inside the store, they formed an orderly line, speaking in low voices, as if they were in church. Indeed, the Marseillais Department Store was almost as grand as a church, with its high vaulted ceilings and checkered marble floors. The delicatessen was a harvest festival of deliciousness laid out in a side chapel—yellow cheeses as large as collection plates, and great organ pipes of sausage dangling at the back. It was also crypt cool, and there was nobody behind the counter.

The water ran down out of their clothes and formed a pool on the checkered marble. The umbrella—which proved to be a parasol—began to drop sodden shreds of dyed paper pulp. Assistants at the dried-flower and pastry counters looked across disapprovingly at these shabby invaders. But they did not offer to serve. Nobody did.

The line of people began to shiver. The delicious array of quiche, pâté, olives, and giant hams was making them hungrier than ever. Each pointed to the kind of sausage they liked best, and said how thick they would ask for it to be cut:

"Every slice a mouthful, that's my style!"

"Oh, I prefer mine wafer thin! It feels like more."

But still nobody came to serve them. Pepper handed out the little macaroons the Malays had given him. Ten minutes passed. A teacher took out her knitting.

"We must get back before the fire brigade," said the woman with Pepper's parasol. "Otherwise they'll think they've won!"

They discussed buying a loaf of bread and sharing it. But as demonstrators, they had developed a stubborn streak not normally in them. They had set their hearts on sliced sausage and would not—could not—turn their backs on the idea.

"We're not stylish enough to serve, that's what," complained a secretary.

"The rich live to eat and the workers eat to live," mused a student of politics.

"We won't eat at all if someone doesn't come soon," said a housekeeper joining the line.

After her came a banker, banging on the counter with his rolled-up newspaper, as if to say, *Serve me, I'm a busy man!* He then rattled open his paper and used it as a wall to separate him from the disheveled folk in front of him in the line. A late news item on the back page caught Pepper's eye:

Ship Lost in Biscay
FRENCH COASTER FOUNDERS

It was Captain Roux's doing; Pepper knew it. *His* doing. He looked down at his braidless jacket and noticed a darker patch near the cuff where Roche's blood had stained it, and his whole body blushed with shame. He wanted to shake himself like a dog: throw off his borrowed identity like water drops. That shining silver meat slicer over there reminded him of the guillotine. There was even a splatter of bright crimson on the wall behind it. His crime weighed on him like scrap iron. The wickedness of it impaled him like a rusty iron fence. The pain was almost unbearable.

Pepper ducked under the counter, took off his jacket, and hung it on the apron hook.

"You work here?" said the woman with the parasol.

"I do now."

"About time!" said the banker.

"Should you be doing that?" asked the secretary.

"Ten slices of chorizo cut good and thick," said a clerk with inky lips.

"The knobbly green one for me," said the teacher with the knitting. "Wafer thin."

Pepper bent his body over the spinning guillotine blade. *Scuff, rip, crack* went the great silver blade into the flesh of each giant sausage; the crowd watched, greedily spellbound, as it sliced and slashed its way through meat, peppercorns, and fat. They winced as Pepper's fingers came closer and closer to the blade. When the greaseproof paper below was piled high with curled petals of deliciousness, he folded it inside another plain, white wrapper and presented it on the palms of both hands. The people in the line gave him a little round of applause.

In this way, Pepper Roux stepped out of his father's unwearable, unbearable life and into the empty space behind the delicatessen counter of the Marseillais Department Store. Nobody really noticed: Their attention was diverted by the whirling silver blade and their rumbling hunger.

Well, people see what they expect, don't they?

Or do they see what they choose?

"Pepper salami," demanded the banker without a smile or a *please*.

"That's me," said the boy behind the counter.

FOUR

PEPPER SALAMI

Every day, Pepper read the newspapers for word of *L'Ombrage*, for further details of the sinking, for news of survivors. But ships sink all the time, and other news floods in, like sea into a hold. *L'Ombrage* was soon lost under a thousand fathoms of newer news, and Pepper could find no mention of Berceau or the engineer, of Gombert, of Annecy or the Duchess.

Suzanne-of-the-delicatessen-counter returned to work next day, her hand hugely bandaged where she had sliced off two fingers on the meat slicer in a moment's carelessness. She did not question why Pepper had taken her place behind the counter: She supposed the management was within its rights to give away her job while she was at the hospital, and the boy plainly had talent. She hovered, tried to make herself useful, tried to help, like a magician's assistant.

Pepper, for his part, waited for Suzanne to tell him that he was not needed and to go away. When she did not, he assumed that he was her assistant and she his senior. He never dreamed that he had robbed her of her crown, her status, her realm of cured meats and cheese.

The floor manager did not query Pepper's presence: Why would anyone turn up and work unless management had employed them? Nobody does anything for nothing. If Pepper had tried to draw wages, then he would have been found out at once. But he did not.

Well, he did pay himself a *kind* of wage: Every evening, he cut himself twelve rounds of salami, each about the size of a coin, and helped himself to a handful of olives, like small change. Each evening, the Bakery department cleared its shelves of perfectly good bread, and this completed Pepper's supper.

After spending one terrifying night sleeping in an alley, he resolved never to do it again. So when six o'clock came, and everyone else laid dust covers over their counters and went home, Pepper did not leave the store. Instead, he migrated to the Soft Furnishings department and slept there, in a splendid double bed, under a sheepskin rug.

A penny candle lent him enough light to read the day's newspapers, which he gathered from the waste cans in the top-floor offices. Word by word, column by column, Pepper scanned news of wars and murders, scandals and road accidents. He read the business pages (though they made no sense); the sports results (though his mother had never let him play rough sports); reviews of exhibitions and concerts (though he had never been to either a concert or an art gallery). He studied the advertisements and the cartoons, the births and the marriages.

But he saved the obituaries till last.

Then he would look for the names of his friends aboard *L'Ombrage*, before finally looking for his own name—(Roux, not Salami)—hoping and dreading he would find it. If the death of Captain Roux was announced, would his mother read it and think she was a widow? Or would his father read it, leap to his feet, and shout, "It's a damned lie!" Aunt Mireille was probably even now scanning the Births, Deaths, &

Marriages section, still hoping for proof that *le pauvre* had kept his appointment with the saints.

And do the saints read the newspaper too, Pepper wondered? Do the angels sit around, like taxi drivers between fares, browsing through news of wars and epidemics, checking the obituaries for some poor soul they have accidentally missed? Could they be fooled? Was it worth a try? Pepper toyed with the idea of posting a notice of his death in the newspapers.

He ought to place an announcement about Roche, at least, he thought, taking the unmailed letter from his jacket pocket:

> Dear Madame Roche,
>   I am very sorry in deed to tell you . . . I did not no him very well, but I expect you did. I am sure he is happy with the saints.

Pepper corrected his spelling mistakes. Reading the newspaper had brought one great benefit: His spelling was getting better.

Lying back on the big bed at night, Pepper was confronted by a maze of brass tubes crisscrossing the ceiling. There were no cash registers in the Marseillais Department Store. Whenever a customer paid, the money was placed in a brass canister, the canister inserted into a tube, and the canister, at the tug of a handle, shot by compressed air along this maze of overhead tubing. It traveled far, far away, to a tiny cage where a cashier took out the money, replaced it with a receipt and any change, and sent it whizzing back through the labyrinth of pipes.

For reasons of hygiene, there was no cash tube in the delicatessen—customers paid at nearby Dry Goods. So after the store shut, Pepper made up for lost time, running from department to department, firing canisters from everywhere to everywhere else, like an artillery barrage. It was the best fun in the world! He imagined how it would feel to be the size of a mouse and climb inside one of those canisters and be rocketed along at heart-stopping speed—around bends and corners, over the heads of customers and shop assistants, unseen, undetected but for a rattle and a musical sigh like a swanny whistle.

Downstairs, the night watchman heard the noise and pushed back his chair, reaching for his keys and his nightstick—then hesitated. What intruder, what burglar, would be using the overhead conveyor system? Why would he? There was only one explanation: ghosts. One-time shop assistants, long-dead cashiers must be the cause of those eerie whizzes and thumps. And a nightstick is useless against the restless dead. The night watchman crossed himself and sat down again.

As Pepper ran from room to room, he pondered: What if pipes like this could be built on an intercontinental scale, to carry money not just from Lingerie to Accounts, but from Paris to Ceylon, where poor people needed it more! Or wages from sailors to their distant wives and children! Or love letters from sweethearts separated by Fate! Letters home from runaway children apologizing for not yet being . . .

Confessions! Yes, yes! If holy confession could be made this way, then Pepper would have been able to write out his three times a week and set it flying to his parish priest! Father Ignatius would unscrew the canister, read the confession inside—

Father, forgive me for
  missing communion

> *not honoring my parents*
> *stealing a ship and twelve rounds of sausage*
> *being fourteen*

—then send forgiveness back wrapped in a sheet of penances:

> *Say three Hail Marys and a novena and don't swim for half an hour after eating sausage.*

Lying back on the big bed, floating between awake and asleep, Pepper continued to muse over the amazing maze of pipes. . . . What about prayers! With enough tubing, you might even reach all the way to Heaven! Oh!

This last idea wedged in his head, in the way all superstition does, and he had to get up and do it, then and there. That night and obsessively each night after, he unscrewed a cash canister in Leather Goods or Horology or Books and slipped a prayer inside it. Then he would tug the brass handle. The cash tube gave a sigh and a rattle, and Pepper's prayer shot off across the ceiling of the Marseillais Department Store like a shooting star through space:

Bless Mother and Aunty, and teach Father to
drink tea.
Please don't make me go yet: I like it here.
Amen.

He never received an answer, and he was very afraid it might jog the saints' memory and put them on his scent again, like bloodhounds. But he could not help himself. Praying each night was one of the rules Aunt Mireille had thrashed into him, and Pepper was a stickler for obeying rules.

Whatever God, in His cashier's cage, thought of Pepper, the customers of the Marseillais Department Store loved him. He sliced sausage and carved ham with more panache than Cyrano de Bergerac, his long knife flashing like a duellist's rapier. He diced with Death at the slicing machine, paring sausages all the way down to their knotted ends with never a care for his fingertips. He ran the deadly cheese wire through cheeses like God separating night from day. He remembered the preferences of all his regulars and pitted all the olives himself, for fear the elderly might choke or break their teeth on the stones. Within a fortnight, he was a celebrity. Well, that is to say, a few regular customers came to know his face, and smile when he served them.

Old Madame Froissart, for instance. Madame Froissart had arthritis in her hands and could no longer crack nuts. So when Suzanne arrived at work each morning—however early she arrived—she found Pepper, sleeves rolled up, shelling walnuts especially for Madame Froissart.

"Where did you work before this?" Suzanne asked, idly fingering his discarded jacket. "On the ships?"

"Not me," said Pepper Salami.

Suzanne was impressed by Pepper's hard work, but not by his physique and crumpled clothes. Suzanne was in love with a boy called Bertrand in Leather Goods. But she had lost two fingers to the meat slicer, and now she would never win Bertrand's heart. This was the conclusion Suzanne had come to, sitting in the hospital, and even when the bandages came off, she could no more pick up her old hopes and dreams than she could pick up a coin from the floor. Bertrand was lost to her, just like her queenly realm: the Delicatessen department.

Pepper also knew about Bertrand in Leather Goods. It was impossible to spend one day with Suzanne without knowing about Bertrand in Leather Goods. Suzanne talked about the shape of his eyebrows, the breadth of his shoulders, the cut of his jacket, his liking for licorice and bicycles, his genius regarding all things leather. . . .

Pepper remembered the romantic novels in his father's study at home. It had always puzzled him why the people in the books loved their sweethearts "hopelessly," "secretly," "from afar" and had to eat their hearts out for three hundred pages before the happy ending put them out of their misery. Why didn't they just say straight out to each other, on page 1, *I love you*? Why did Suzanne not just walk over to Bertrand and say, *I really admire your eyebrows and how much you know about leather—let's get married*? Pepper could see for himself that she was kind of pretty and pretty kind. If it had not been for the calluses on his knees (and being overdue in the death department), who knows?—he might have fallen in love with her himself. But people ought not waste time. If there was one thing Aunt Mireille's dream had taught him, it was not to waste precious time.

So one evening, he borrowed the keys from the top-floor offices, let himself into a cashier's booth, slipped a note into a canister—*Suzanne loves you, Bertrand*—and sent it, like Cupid's arrow, across the ceiling and down to Leather Goods on the floor below. Then he went back to bed and lay there imagining the happy effect next day.

Except that suddenly, the idea had sprung a leak. And the more he thought about it, the more leaks it sprang. What if Bertrand already had a girlfriend? What if he did not like brunettes? What if he was planning to be a priest? What if he showed the note to his fellow leather experts and they laughed about it together? What if word got out and the whole store began to point and smirk and jeer . . . ? Hot with panic, Pepper hurried back to the cashier's booth and wrote, on the backs of a dozen Marseillais Department Store receipt slips: *Philippe loves Marguerite. Jean adores Annette. Pomme wants to marry Guillaume. As pants the hart after water, so pants Henri after Fleur.* (That one sounded a bit strong, but it came from the Bible, so it must be all right.) *Hercule sends a kiss to Nanette. Claude loves Gisele.* He tried to think of every staff member he knew by name, tried to leave nobody out, for fear they should feel unloved. In every tube a message. In every department a mysterious note declaring love, devotion, or heartache. It would have been nice to include himself—*Somebody-or-other loves Pepper Salami*—but that was carrying fiction too far, what with his knees. Anyway, there was no cash tube in the Delicatessen department. Only when he had tugged the last handle and all the pipes had fallen silent overhead did his own heart quiet enough for him to return to bed.

Downstairs, meanwhile, the night watchman scribbled a note of his own, resigning his job at the Marseillais Department Store effective immediately, *On account of the unholy creatures rampaging around up top.*

Next morning, Pepper overslept. He woke to the sound of voices on either side of the bed. A woman's hand took hold of the sheepskin and lifted it clear of Pepper's head. He opened his eyes and found the husband's face on a level with his own, peering at him.

"I'm an advertisement," said Pepper in a bleating whisper. "A Dormieux bed is better than counting sheep. . . ."

Except that I fell asleep. Just shows. Very good bed. Can't keep awake. Would you like to try it?" And clasping the sheepskin rug around his shoulders and face, he gathered up his shoes, jacket, and tie and trotted away to the back stairs. The departmental assistant—already at his counter—should have seen him and ranted. But he was too busy reading a note he had just found inside the cash canister.

As the hours passed, the cavernous department store filled up with an atmosphere as volatile as gasoline fumes. The least spark, and it seemed the whole place would explode. A young man fainted in Arts and Crafts. A matron in Linens needed smelling salts. Fleur from Floristry gathered up her skirts, climbed to the fourth floor, and slapped Henri in Shoes & Boots, declaring, "I'm a married woman, you panting beast!" Unfortunately, by the time she returned to her counter, all the day's fresh red roses, newly delivered from the market, had disappeared, pilfered by a raiding party of counter assistants and a cashier or two. The Perfume department enjoyed a sudden run on eau de cologne and pomade, but sales were down in other departments, chiefly because there was no one there to serve customers. Assistants had abandoned their posts. The Marseillais Department Store prided itself on employing only the most proper, genteel, and respectable staff, but in unscrewing their little brass canisters, it was as if they had loosed laughing gas: By lunchtime hysteria had gained the upper hand.

The phonograph in Music and Musical Instruments usually played the *Moonlight* Sonata endlessly to lure in passing customers. Today it played Felix Mayol singing "Amour de Trottin" in the pitch-dark basement bistro, and couples danced on the unlit dance floor to the crackle of dust on the wax cylinder and the static electricity in their hearts.

Suzanne simply wept. All her worst fears had been proved right. Nobody could possibly love a woman maimed by a slicing machine. Nobody had sent her a note.

"But we don't *have* a cash tube in the deli!" Pepper tried to tell her. "If we had, you would have gotten a note, I'm sure!"

But Suzanne only sat, her damaged hand cradled against her chest, and rocked to and fro, weeping for her lost opportunities.

Then, suddenly, Bertrand arrived at the counter like a debt collector. He was wearing a flat, black leather cap that made him look fifty. In one hand he carried a pair of patent leather dance pumps he had "borrowed" from Shoes & Boots, in the other a stolen rose almost as crimson as his face. "There's music in the downstairs," he said belligerently.

"There is?" asked Suzanne, rising as though on the updraft of it.

"Yes."

"Lovely."

"So . . ."

"Lovely!"

And away they went, oblivious to Pepper, or the possibility of customers or even complete sentences.

In Butchery there was no cash tube either, but rumor had been carried there all the same, by compressed air. Rumor said that the butcher's wife Fleur had received romantic advances from Henri in Shoes. Christophe the butcher went in search of Henri with a meat saw.

So there was no one in Butchery to take delivery of the game birds that arrived weekly from a local estate. Pepper ran over to do it, and the gamekeeper's boy emptied the sacks at his feet—an avalanche of shot pheasants, limp and ruffled, eyes staring, claws dangling. At the sight of them tumbling out onto the floor, Pepper felt pure horror. As ill omens go, what could be iller than twenty brace of glassy-eyed pheasants piling up around your ankles?

Management, scenting the fumes of passion, came sniffing across the shop floor. "Where is Christophe, the butcher?"

"Haunching a deer," said Pepper, quick as a wink.

"Where is . . . er . . . the girl? With the hand."

"Suzanne? Helping an old lady to carry things to the tram, sir," said Pepper, feeling the lies condense into sweat on his forehead, and a taste in his mouth like soap. If his Final Hour really had come, and angels were even now parking their fiery chariots on the roof of the Marseillais Department Store, they ought not to find him busy telling lies. The spongy flesh and clicking claws of the dead pheasants pressed against his legs and feet.

"What's that music I can hear?" said Management.

"A customer wanted a demonstration of the phonograph, sir. There's one too many pheasants, sir; would you like it?" And wrapping up a bird in pristine white paper, Pepper gave it to Mr. Management to be rid of him. Pepper was left with feathers clinging to his cuffs—left, too, with the memory of the purple tongue poking through a little crossed beak, the warning in those pheasant eyes: *Run! Get away! You'll end up like us! You think you're all the colors of happiness—doing no harm to anyone—then suddenly one day . . .*

Bang! Something struck Pepper on the back. Pellets of fear and guilt lodged throughout his body.

"You took my girl's job," snarled Bertrand from Leather Goods, thumping Pepper again with his black leather cap. "Suzie says you took her job while she was at the hospital. That right?"

"I suppose. . . ."

"So now you're going to give it up, ain't you!"

Suzanne loitered in the background, holding a nosegay of violets, biting her lip but smiling despite herself. She had not asked Bertrand to take up her cause—had only mentioned it in passing. But she could not help delighting in Bertrand—so manly, so fierce!—ousting her usurper like some knight-errant in patent leather shoes.

Henri from Shoes & Boots sped by, protesting his innocence, pursued by Christophe and his meat saw.

"You going or what?" asked Bertrand, and slapped Pepper with his cap again.

"Yes, but first I have to explain to Christophe!"

"I'll do that!" cheeped Suzanne, feet still dancing to the music inside her head. She ran and fetched Pepper's jacket from the apron hook. It seemed the best way to save his life, and she had nothing personal against Pepper himself. "Explain what?"

"About his wife and Henri. It isn't true! It was me! I didn't know she was married!"

The butcher, just then doubling back to cut Henri off at Confectionery, heard Pepper and blundered to a halt, misunderstanding—"You wrote love letters to my wife?"—then simply hurled the saw at Pepper where he stood mired in a swamp of dead pheasants.

Feathers, tendons, and claws; feathers, beaks, and eyes: They filled Pepper's vision as he dived out of the path of the saw, sliding on his face across the check-ered floor. Christophe picked him up by the shoulders of his jacket, dragged him to the great silver meat slicer—"You been cozying up to my Fleur?"—and set its circular guillotine blade spinning. Pepper's flailing hands groped for the carving knife but found only the bowl of olive stones he had gouged out of the olives that morning, tipping them over, scattering the floor of the delicatessen with pits and broken china. Christophe lost his footing.

"Excuse me!" called Madame Froissart's frail, piping voice from beyond the counter. "I say, excuse me! I've come for my nuts."

And Pepper fled, scrabbling for purchase with the toes of his boots, skidding on the fruits of his own kindness, fleeing through the revolving doors, out onto the sunny street. A tram was passing, and he pitched himself at it and clung to its coachwork, face pressed to the painted metal as to the scalding funnel of *L'Ombrage*.

The tram carried him past a war memorial to the Crimean dead, topped by a bronze angel, wings outspread. Pepper looked up at the angel now with rage and resentment. Every day for a month, he had worked with sharp blades, wires, and guillotines—expressly allowing the saints a fair chance to spill his blood. Was it quite necessary, then, for the angels to employ Bertrand from Leather Goods and a jealous butcher as assassins? Christophe, perhaps—but *Bertrand*? In his stupid leather cap? If the saints wanted to humiliate Pepper as well as assassinate him, they would have to try harder and run faster next time.

Outside the town hall, the tram turned left, and Pepper was jolted free of his handholds, tumbling into the street. He half expected the fire brigade to be there to hose him down. But there was no demonstration today, no sign of civil discontent—only a single rain-smeared placard propped up against a horse trough. It said:

DOWN WITH THE HONGRIOT-PLEUVIEZ AMENDMENT (CLAUSE 5)!

Pepper caught the coastal train to Abaron. Its wheels—huge and remorseless as a dozen meat slicers—sliced the journey into wafer-thin petals of time that fell away into the dust, never to be recovered. Taking off his jacket in the hot carriage, he found a ragged tear in the sleeve—so either the saw or the meat slicer had caught him, after all. There was a matching bruise on his arm. It was time to change lives again; time to slice Pepper Salami so wafer thin that the light would shine through—time to slice him invisible.

FIVE

NEWSPEPPER

"Someone's dead," said Pepper, and immediately felt better.

"Fill in the form," said the woman behind the counter of the *Étoile Sud* newspaper offices.

And so Pepper announced his own death, not so much for the benefit of any taxicab angels browsing through the paper, or even his aunt Mireille, but more to convince himself that *le pauvre* was indeed dead to the world. He was no longer Paul Roux and never would be again. *Maybe you'll leave me alone now,* he found himself thinking.

The woman behind the counter saw him struggling to fit all his words onto the form. "That'll cost you," she said. "Words don't come cheap."

"What about the free press?" asked Pepper, who had heard of it and thought it meant you didn't have to pay.

"Nothing's free in this life. Put your head out the window and shout—there's free speech. Us you pay for," said the woman, snatching back the form and crumpling it up. "In here it costs two francs a line." She had a face like a dishcloth being wrung out. Pepper thought she must spend too much time reading about tragedies in the newspaper.

When he grasped that it cost money to put a death notice in the newspaper, he asked for another form and rewrote his entry in as few words as possible, paying with one of the notes rolled up in his pocket.

ROUX, Paul
formerly of
Bois-sous-Clochet
Drowned at sea 11 July.
Sadly missed.
"The sea shall
give up her dead"

"Gone to Glory's cheaper," said the woman, so he changed the quote, though it seemed a terrible lie. He

crossed through *Sadly missed* as well. That probably wasn't true either. Besides, he still had to pay for the announcement about Roche.

Presumably the shipping company would no longer be sending Roche's wages to his widow, knowing full well the ship was on the ocean bed. So there was no longer any point in pretending he was alive. Roche's wife *needed* to know she was a widow, and he had not plucked up the courage to notify her. Was it kind to let her read about her husband's death in the paper? Well that depended on what she read, didn't it?

Pepper could not say that Roche had gone down with the ship, because then she would start having the same dreams as Pepper: terrible, terrible dreams. . . . No, Claude Roche deceased must be all the things Claude Roche alive could have been if he had tried harder (and if he hadn't been such a natural-born pig).

"Someone else died," he said, and the woman pursed her lips but gave him a third form to fill in.

He wrote of the death of one Claude Roche of Aigues Mortes, a seaman who, having newly escaped a shipwreck, heroically sacrificed his life while on a visit to the Marseille zoo. Seeing a child fall into the lion pit, he had unhesitatingly thrown himself in too, as an alternative meal for the lions. Lifting the child onto his shoulders, he had been able to pass her into the arms of her mother before the lions attacked. Pepper even afforded Roche a "Sadly missed" as well as a "Gone to Glory." The notice cost a small fortune.

A door opened behind the woman, and noise burst through from the print rooms. Pepper glimpsed the presses—giant cylinders, windmill paddles wafting huge sheets of newsprint. A man entered in shirtsleeves and a beret; the woman's eager smile and fluttering hands said that here was the editor.

The editor of *L'Étoile Sud* was no good at listening or at looking people in the face, but he gobbled up the written word wherever he found it. He had clearly also heard that words cost money, because he was constantly in search of them. He sipped and sucked them up— off tickets, public notices, other shop signs, matchboxes, food packaging, and calendars. After glancing through the day's mail, he let his eyes stray along the counter, reading advertisements and announcement forms:

"*. . . three cob mares sound in wind and limb . . .*"

"*. . . to Godet-Dupont a son 5 pounds . . .*"

90

". . . *Lebec-Belot at the Church of the Bleeding Heart . . .*"

"*Limoges, Albert, suddenly at home, aged 89. Gone to Glory.*"

Unsatisfied, his eyes came to rest on the death notice Pepper had just filled in. Snatching it up, he turned the form this way and that to read the extra words written up the sides for lack of space: . . . *placing himself between the ravening beasts and the child . . .*

"Did we cover this? I don't remember us covering this? Who posted this? A relation? Local? Did we cover this story?"

Pepper was all set to creep away, but the woman pointed him out as the culprit.

"What are you? A relation?" demanded the editor.

"No," said Pepper.

"There's a story here, isn't there? A good story?"

"Oh yes, sir, probably," said Pepper, who hated to disappoint.

"How come you're posting the death, then?" The questions were sharp and aggressive, like a hand pushing him in the chest. Pepper retreated, starting to panic. What if an *Étoile* journalist went to the Marseille zoo and asked about the man in the lion pit? Pepper was not even sure Marseille *had* a zoo.

The editor picked up a telephone and wound a handle beside it. "Who's free to do a story in Marseille?"

"I am!" blurted Pepper, and then, when the editor paid no attention: "I'll write it!"

"You?" said the editor, absently browsing through the telephone bill and an invoice for staples.

"Why wouldn't I?" said Pepper. He was starting to get the journalistic hang of this talking in questions.

"You're a journalist?"

"Would I offer if I weren't?"

"What've you done before?"

"What haven't I?" But that came out sounding cocky, so Pepper quickly added, "You remember that Hongriot-Pleuviez Amendment? A scandal . . . particularly clause five."

The editor coughed and ran a finger around the collar of his shirt. Studiously he read a dropped shopping list and bus ticket lying on the floor. "You covered that story?"

"Didn't you?" said Pepper.

"Freelance?"

"Yes and no," said Pepper, who had no idea what it

meant but liked the sound of the *lance*.

"Who do you work for right now?" said the editor, reading the maker's label inside Pepper's jacket.

"For you, sir, don't I?" said Pepper. And found that he did.

Well, people see what they look for, don't they? And people who never look at their fellow men get what they deserve. Thus Pepper stepped into *L'Étoile Sud*, a silo of words, hoping the words would close over him like grain and bury him from sight.

They found him a desk and asked him to fill seventy-five column inches each week with news-worthy stories. The other journalists peered toward him through dense palls of cigarette smoke, screwing shut their eyes. The paper was losing money: Maybe the editor was bringing in younger, cheaper men, to save on wages.

Pepper had no idea how to fill seventy-five column inches. He only knew that he did not want *his* stories to be as depressing as all the ones he had read by candle-light, in bed, in the Marseillais Department Store. First he wrote up the story of Claude Roche, making it even more racy and heroic than before, throwing in a dying wish for good measure: *Roche was heard to shout, before the lions attacked, "Tell my wife I love her!"*

And after that, he wrote the kind of stories he would himself have liked to read, curled up under the sheepskin rug in the Soft Furnishings department. Take Henri Leclerc, who won nine thousand francs in the lottery and so was able to marry his childhood sweetheart:

Cont'd from p. 4

Said Mr. Leclerc, brushing the rice from the shoulders of his fashionable Paris suit: "Before my good luck, Fleur's parents would drive me from their door, throwing plant pots and tennis rackets, and shouting, 'Begone! You are far too poor! Our daughter deserves better!' I was severely injured on several occasions."

The bride told *L'Étoile Sud*: "I always knew love would find a way. We were willing to wait a hundred years to be together, but we are glad we did not have to."

The couple are honeymooning in Japan.

By PEPPER PAPIER

TREASURE TROVE IN SECRET BAY

MARSEILLE—A wooden chest containing priceless pirate treasure has been found by vacationers in shallow water off the Provençal coast. The sea chest, thought to have fallen overboard from a Turkish galley in the thirteenth century, contains gold plunder and gemstones big as pigeon eggs, according to an eyewitness. The find also includes an embalmed parrot. "Stomach of bird is full of doubloons," said Professor Euclid Valparaiso. "We investigate possibility is—how you say?—hush money."

The find will be studied, and then shared among the friends who found it. The exact position of the cove is being kept a close secret, to foil would-be treasure hunters.

By PEPPER PAPIER

MAN THOUGHT DEAD RETURNS FROM WAR

QUOMBIER—A soldier thought to have died in the Siege of Paris returned to his home in the tiny hamlet of Quombier last Wednesday.

Paul Blois, thought to have died in the siege, astonished friends and relations when he rode into the village on a bicycle.

"I thought I was seeing a ghost," stated Manon Ballon, 41, "but he was smoking a pipe, so I knew I wasn't."

Paul's mother, Aimée, 91, remarked: "He has changed somewhat, but I knew him at once. He is my boy. I said all along he was not gone. I would have known if my little boy was dead."

Paul's fiancée, Mireille, was so upset by reports of her fiancé's "death" that she never

Cont'd on p. 12

TODAY'S CHILDREN MORE AGREEABLE, SAYS GOVERNMENT REPORT

OSLO—Young people are kinder and more charming than fifty years ago, says a shock report issued by the Norwegian government yesterday. The latest statistics have shown that children do not steal, fight, talk back or tell lies as much as their grandparents did.

Though others dispute his results, Dr. Gustav Guberson of Oslo University claims that better food and more churchgoing have "turned our young folk into good citizens." The words "thank you" and "please" are used more than 80,000 times during the average child-

Cont'd on p. 21

"Where's Quombier?" called the typesetter from the door of the setting room. "I never heard of it."

"Eight houses, two barns, and a water mill," replied Pepper at once, because, in his head (if not in person), he had been to Quombier and interviewed Paul Blois and his ancient mother and joyful fiancée. He had shared in their happiness, even though, *strictly speaking*, these people did not exist.

He made them up. Every last one of them. He invented their names and their ages—even sometimes their villages. He invented their tremendous good luck or selfless bravery, their goodness, and their marvelous adventures. Like little flares they were lit one by one, to brighten up the lives of *L'Étoile*'s readers and to make them feel that perhaps, after all, the world was not as bleak and lonely and angry and scary and hard as they feared.

As he feared.

SEA MONSTER IS DECLARED EXTINCT

PARIS—The kraken, once the terror of every ship's crew, has been officially declared extinct. The Institute of Marine Biology in Paris yesterday announced that the heavy shipping of recent years has emptied the oceans of all giant squid.

A spokesman said, "We have seen the last of these dangerous, destructive pests. They will be eating no more ships from now on."

By PEPPER PAPIER

Like the cash canisters in the Marseillais Department Store, Pepper fired his stories off into space and saw them—miraculously!—appear in print between the advertisements for hair oil and chest rub, between accounts of war atrocities and reports of murder trials and escaped convicts roaming the countryside. The chief copy editor put them into better French (because copy editors cannot read anything without changing it), so Pepper was able to read them afresh when they were printed, and feel proud—to share in the happiness of his invented characters all over again. Pepper planted his stories around like little night-lights to keep nightmares away. Because, he reasoned, the readers almost certainly suffered nightmares.

Just like his.

Pepper dreamed of a giant squid embracing *L'Ombrage*. He dreamed of Roche beckoning, beckoning, calling out to him, through bloodied lips and two thousand fathoms of water: *Throw down a line! Pull me back up!* He dreamed of being driven in a tumbrel toward a guillotine like a giant meat slicer; of wading waist deep among soft, decaying pheasants toward a hangman's gallows. At the foot of the gallows steps stood his father, holding a noose and a placard, protesting about his son's crimes. At his shoulder stood Aunt Mireille, looking at her pocket watch, its ticking so loud that it drowned out Pepper's excuses. He dreamed that the fire brigade was hosing him down with ink, indelible ink, and that ink-black rooks, as thickly strewn as the pheasants, were stuffing up the sky, blocking out the sun. Time and again they would swoop down and slash at his face, trying to pull it away, trying to see who he was under the mask. . . .

"This piece about the creature that's been discovered, Papier . . . ," said the editor.

"With the rainbow fur, sir?"

"With the rainbow fur. And a taste for . . . what was it again?"

"Crows, sir."

"Crows, yes."

"And candles."

"And candles."

"And household rubbish, sir."

The editor's insatiable eyes trailed over Pepper's latest article. "Do you have any pictures?"

"No pictures—no, sir."

"Pictures would help, Papier. A photograph."

"I could describe it to the designer man and he could sketch one, sir."

"If you knew what one looked like."

"I could guess, sir."

The editor's eyes opened very, very wide. His complexion darkened. "You do realize, Papier, that the public looks to us for *fact*. Absolute factually accurate, factual *fact*. The buying public cannot abide . . . *fiction*. The buying public detests *fiction*." When he said it, his lips drew back from his front teeth as if he might, at any moment, spit the word back out again into a handkerchief and throw it in the trash. His eyes swerved to and fro now across the surface of his desk: an invoice for paper; Pepper's article on the rainbowy lemurs raiding trash cans in Avignon; a child's drawing of "Daddy." They came to rest on the latest circulation figures of the newspaper, and there they stopped. For he saw, to his astonishment, that sales of *L'Étoile Sud* had actually risen ten percent in the last month. Advertising revenue was up eighteen percent. It was inexplicable: *L'Étoile Sud* had been on a downward slide for years. The editor shook himself, shut his gaping mouth, and thumped the desk.

"Give me something meaty, Papier. Something weighty. Something *verifiable* before the end of the week, or I'm sorry, but I'll just have to . . ." He let the threat hang in the air, unspoken. "Give me some cold

hard facts, man! News, man! I'm killing the lemurs."
And he crushed the article into a ball and threw it in the
trash without once resting his eyes on its author. Then
and there, Pepper's rainbow-colored lemurs ceased to
exist. Amazing how a living creature could be bounding around one moment and extinct the next.

Pepper was frightened. He liked being a journalist. He
liked spread-eagling himself on the paper bales where
he slept at night, like a pencil-drawn stick figure. He
liked reading his own (invented) name in the newspaper. If he did not think about the taste, he liked the
pies his fellow journalists never finished at lunchtime.
Above all, he loved sweeping together words—like
dead flies from a windowsill—onto a sheet of white
paper and seeing them come to life: events! characters!
places! living, breathing news. . . .

He had no idea how to go out and find a *true* news
story—something that had really occurred. Everything that happened out there—outside the street
doorway—was cruel, dangerous, or sad: You only
had to read the newspapers to know that. Murders.
Fights. Thefts. Dangerous prisoners on the run.

Train crashes. Arson. Anyway . . .

Anyway. By now angels might be lurking around any and every corner, collars turned up, stiletto knives in their pockets. Saints were probably stopping boys in the street, demanding to see their identity cards, bundling them into the backs of black vans or flaming chariots. But if Pepper stayed put and had to write the truth, there was only one truly newsworthy story he knew—and that was untouchable.

It hung in his head like a hornet's nest, that story, that secret, that piece of knowledge. For weeks it had buzzed between his ears, stung the backs of his eyes until the tears ran down. What a relief it would be to write it, to put it on the outside for a change; to turn it outdoors along with the nightmares. So, threatened with losing his job, his home, his identity, his sanity, Pepper Papier wrote down the story of *L'Ombrage*'s last voyage. He started out not knowing how to begin. He came to the end not knowing how to stop. He wrote it rocking forward and back in his chair so savagely that the journalists and copy editors stopped clattering at their typewriters and watched. He wrote it crying so hard that his jacket cuffs were soaked and the paper crinkled like seersucker. Looking up, Pepper saw them staring and blushed scarlet.

"The lemur story's dead," he said. "He killed my lemurs."

Then he went to crumple up his article about the coffin ship *L'Ombrage*. Of course he could not *really* allow the newspaper to print it. There would be Hell to pay. And Aunt Mireille had taught him all about Hell.

As his hand closed over the pages, another closed over his; a hand twice the size. The editor had been standing behind him, reading over his shoulder. And, after twenty-five years as a hack journalist, the editor knew a good story when he saw one.

What the editor had been looking for was an excuse to fire Pepper. (He liked firing people.) What he got was a scoop. First he scrutinized every word, looking to find fault. (He liked to find fault—almost as much as he liked firing people.) Tugging the sheets of paper from Pepper's grip, he combed through each sentence, looking for signs of invention, of *fiction*. But though the spelling was erratic, and the pencil handwriting hard to read, the content was both sensational and precise. It even contained the chart position at which *L'Ombrage* had been deliberately scuppered in midocean, taking with it one seaman, a steward, and the captain. *The fate of everybody else is unknown*, read the last line.

Oh yes, there was one fiction the editor had failed to spot. Pepper had allowed Captain Roux to repent his crimes and go down with his ship. Captain Pepper was dead. Now it had to be true. It was in the newspaper.

"It's a couple of months old," said the editor grudgingly, "but it'll do. Find out where the captain lived and get the grieving-widow angle."

A picture came into Pepper's head, then, of a dozen journalists beating at the door of his home—wanting to know, demanding to know—their knocking sending the rooks screaming into the sky. . . .

"The captain wasn't married, sir," said Pepper.

The story was picked up by the national papers and syndicated all over France. Pepper had no idea what *syndicated* meant: All he heard was the *sin* part of it; and Aunt Mireille had taught him everything about the wages of sin.

The owners of Maritime Sud & Cie were asked to comment, but declined and quickly called in their lawyers.

The police arrived at the offices of *L'Étoile Sud*.

Terrified, thinking they had found him out to be Captain Roux of *L'Ombrage*, Pepper jumped up from his desk, meaning to run. Where to run? The only way out of the print rooms was through the front office, and the front office was full of police officers. So he clambered up the iron-runged ladder that rose toward the wrought-iron trusses of the metal roof. Below him the journalists—all fat, lethargic men who moved with the slowness of meat pies—gaped up at him in disbelief.

"Where you going?" called Poulet.

"Don't worry! The boss won't hand you over to the cops!" called Dulac.

But Pepper kept climbing, until he reached the service hatch in the roof and pulled himself through into fresh air, scattering the pigeons that roosted along the roof ridge.

For a moment, the immensity of the sky made his head spin. For a month he had hibernated in the print rooms below, living on words and piecrust and coffee. His heart said that he had been to Quombier and the Marseilles zoo and Beaulieu and Grand Pré and the Church of the Bleeding Heart: meeting people, collecting stories. But the feeble muscles in his arms and legs, the blinding sunlight in his eyes, told him that he had in fact been nowhere for a month. Now he sat down on the steeply sloping corrugated iron roof, clutched his knees to his chest, and wondered what it would be like in prison.

The pigeons looked at him, heads cocked like pistols. The metal of the roof was as hot as a ship's funnel. The sky encircling him was shot with the red of evening, as if the clouds had impaled themselves on the trees and were bleeding into their crumpled shirts. He was fourteen years and thirteen weeks old, and he had not been to confession for ninety days. Was this where his luck ran out? He walked along the roof ridge to the end of the building, but the gap between this and the offices next door was much too wide to jump.

Meanwhile, down in the front office, the editor looked the police squarely in the eye. They asked him where he had gotten his information about the sinking of *L'Ombrage*. He refused point-blank to tell them. He would not—he could not reveal his sources, he said. The establishment could put him up against a wall and shoot him if they wanted: He would protect his sources with his last drop of blood!

For his whole life the editor had wanted to print the kind of story that would bring the police to his door, demanding to know how and where he had found it. He was not going to waste the moment now by telling them.

"So which of your people wrote this article, then?" asked the police sergeant, smacking the offending newspaper with the back of his hand.

"That I cannot tell you! I must protect the identity of both the author and his informant! That is the unwritten law of my profession!" And the editor stood tall and unblinking, secretly hoping the police would think he had written it himself.

The police shuffled their feet, shrugged, and went away. The owners of Maritime Sud & Cie had all been arrested the day before, and were being interrogated about seven deliberate sinkings, seven fraudulent insurance claims. It no longer really mattered just who had snitched on them to the press or who had exposed their crimes in the newspapers for everyone to read about.

"You can come down now, *petite taupe*," called Dulac through cupped hands. "The cops have gone."

Pepper crossed himself and said a Hail Mary. Inside his sun-hot head, an idea had somehow risen, baked and browned: The police were really angels in disguise hunting the runaway Paul Roux. And yet they had gone without catching his scent, without smiting him down, without even circling the roof on triple seraphim wings! He climbed back down into the print rooms, legs shaking; sat at his desk; and, just to celebrate, wrote a story about a chicken in Bagnol that had laid forty-three eggs in one day. Around him the printing machines flailed like windmills, and the giant rollers spewed out page after page of news, cut wafer thin. The chief setter said, "Have you heard? Circulation's up thirty percent. Happy days."

The editor came back from the front office, mopping his forehead with a handkerchief. Laughs, like hiccups, kept breaking free from his throat. "I believe a glass of wine might be in order, gentlemen," he said.

"Go and get us half a dozen bottles of red, will you, Papier?" And he pulled out his wallet.

The heat was dying out of the day, so Pepper put on his jacket to go to the wineshop. His head was full of new ideas for stories: about a parakeet that could translate Malay into French—about a cure for baldness involving marmalade—about a boy who receives a mysterious envelope on his fourteenth birthday, and inside it a fancy iron key to a chateau along with a note saying *I want you to have it. . . .*

So he did not notice the sound of footsteps behind him, keeping pace with his, until he was almost at the shop. Glancing back, he saw the figure of a man stop sharply and lift one finger to point at him. A chill went down Pepper's spine, as if the iron key in the story had been dropped down his collar. The bright lights of the wineshop were comforting and reassuring once he was inside: the rows of wine bottles a palette of glorious oily reds, pinks, greens, and golds. Pepper had never been in such a shop, never bought wine before, and never drunk it except at Holy Communion. He was enchanted by the huge array of shapes perched like statues around a church. The labels bore lilies, portcullises, castles, eagles, boars, rearing horses, and crowns. Some bottles wore little helmets of silver wire, others sackcloth tunics like monks doing penance.

"Six bottles of red, please," said Pepper, and the vintner laughed out loud and spread wide his arms to indicate the choice.

Then someone outside the shop put his face close to the window, hands cupped around the eyes to peer through the glass. Condensation at once blotted out the face, so only the shape of the head showed, hands curving like tusks away from the cheekbones.

Pepper emptied the money out of his fist onto the shop counter. "Sorry. Please. Sorry. Give this back to the editor at *L'Étoile,* will you? Say Papier's sorry, but he had to go." Then he squeezed between the racks of wine, setting them chinking and rocking; forced open the back door of the shop; and tumbled out into an alleyway. The alleyway had only one exit—back onto the main street. As Pepper walked briskly toward the streetlights, the same figure stepped into the alley's opening: a silhouette against the streetlamp, a halo of gaslight around his hat.

"Roux!"

Pepper turned back and ran. He ran at the alley's end wall, dislodging mortar with the toes of his boots, scuffing his knees, reaching up. There was barbed wire along the top of the wall. A clothesline in the garden beyond that caught him in the throat and threw him on his back. But not until Pepper had vaulted three fences did he feel any pain other than fear.

SIX

CONFESSIONS

The best time to get killed is immediately after going to confession. Well, after doing penance, too, of course, but that's the easy part.

A long time ago, Aunty Mireille had explained how the rules worked: If, when he died, Pepper was carrying any unforgiven sins around with him (such as a dirty handkerchief or five out of ten for his math assignment, or second helpings at dinner), he would have to go to Hell and have those sins burned away before he could present himself in Heaven. There was no guarantee he would be allowed into Heaven at all—not after eating cake with his fingers instead of a fork—but while he was larded in sin, there was no point in even trying.

She had said this one day while a leg of pork was roasting over the fire. Together, hand in hand, they had stood and watched the fat run down the roast and drip into the grate, making the flames jump, and Mireille had held his hand so tightly that his knuckles *crunch-crunch*ed inside her fist. "That will be you," she whispered under her breath, "if you don't go to visit Father Ignatius *every* day." Aged six at the time, Pepper had been deeply impressed.

Running and fear made him warm, but midnight turned his sweat to rivulets of cold under his clothes, and he took refuge in a church. Curling up on a pew, he slept like a sardine on a drying rack until, rolling off onto the floor by accident, he discovered a row of little cushions hanging from the pews in front and lined them all up into a bed.

As the first light of day jimmied its way through the stained-glass windows, Pepper parted his eyelids and whimpered. On all sides, saints were emerging from the shadows. Invisible at midnight, a dozen of them stood there now, plainly shocked into stillness at finding Paul Roux on their premises. Gradually other familiar sights loomed out of the gloom—memorials, plaster angels, candle sconces, flower vases, and shining brass—and Pepper surfaced from sleep cramming his terror back into his chest. But a moment later he found himself looking at a banner embroidered by local housewives:

MOTHERS' UNION OF THE CHURCH
OF SAINT CONSTANCE

it said in cross-stitch.

"Damn, damn, damn," said Pepper, though he never ever swore. How could a boy hope to win against such odds? Of all the churches he could have hidden in, he had to pick the one devoted to blessed Saint Constance: the saint who had spoken his doom to Aunty Mireille. He did not believe in coincidences. Whole churches were probably moving around like chess pieces within France, just to demonstrate to him the pointlessness of running, the hopelessness of hope.

So which of the plaster figures was Saint Constance, then? Pepper picked out the statue that looked most like Aunt Mireille and knelt down in front of it.

"Oh, excuse me a minute," he said, and went back to fetch a hassock to kneel on. The church at home did not have these little cushiony things. (And Aunt Mireille would never have let him use them.) But

Pepper could not resist placing one at the saint's feet to protect his poor knees from the chipped stone floor.

"Please, could I—" No, no. He was forgetting his manners. He must not ask for something until he had made the right polite remarks. "Blessed art thou, Saint Constance, and I hope you're well. I have a message for you somewhere. From my aunty." He pulled out the wad of crumpled, torn, dog-eared prayers he had been carrying around for months, and leafed through them for the one addressed to Saint Constance. "I'm sorry. I was supposed to give this to you myself. In person. In Heaven. But just in case I don't . . . for a while . . ." He looked for somewhere to lodge the slip of paper, but statues come in one big lump, and the sculptors never think to give them pockets. Looking around, he saw that the carved eagle holding up the Holy Scriptures was looking at him all too keenly, its glass eyes fixed on him as on a small, edible rabbit.

Quickly, Pepper lit a candle for the Duchess, and another for Roche, then moved the second farther along the candle rack, because Duchesse could never abide Roche, the pig. In between, he lit a candle for his father (in case he was languishing in jail on account of

Pepper's snitching newspaper article). He lit another for his mother—and quickly a fourth for Aunt Mireille, because Aunt Mireille had always held his hand over the candle flames if he forgot this little courtesy. For a moment he thought he could almost feel the burn on his palms, but it was only the holes made by the barbed wire, getting infected. He lit a fifth candle for himself and stuffed a ten-franc note half into the slot because he did not have any small change.

Saint Constance looked down with dull, painted eyes, unimpressed. There were chips in her cheeks and painted hair. Perhaps the blessed saints did not go gray and wrinkly with the passing centuries but simply flaked color. He had meant to ask for a stay of execution—another year or two of being alive. After all, a thousand years is but a day in the eyes of the Lord. He had meant to be abject and terribly, terribly polite. . . .

But the protesters in Marseille had stirred him up inside. Injustice at the Marseillais Department Store had taught him how to feel angry and resentful. And journalism had filled his head with questions. "*Why* do I have to die at fourteen?" he burst out. "Whose idea was it? Was it your idea?"

Saint Constance stared blankly back, not quite meeting his eye. Her chipped red mouth looked as if she had been eating crusty bread and had not licked her lips clean. Duchesse would have licked his lips clean. Duchesse would have said something encouraging.

"Was it your idea? What for? Why fourteen?" He found he had gotten to his feet, ducking his head this way and that to try to make eye contact. But Constance continued to look around him, through him. In sheer vexation, he put out his hands to give her a push. . . . Then a thought: What if she could not see him because he no longer existed?

A door opened, and a draft snuffed out his candles: one, two, three, four—easy as that—leaving only his own flame trembling on its wick. Pepper, still bristling with fright, squirmed back between the pews and lay hidden.

"I've seen no one of that description at all, I fear," the priest was saying as he came in, to someone close behind him. "No one unknown to me. No one to rouse my suspicions. When did he break loose? He'll be making for the wide open. It's common among the prison types—to hide out in the salty places. Or the seaside. It's all strangers and rogues on the seashore these days."

Together the two men walked through the nave, their shoes scuffing stone dust. Pepper wondered who this was, asking about some fugitive ne'er-do-well: the police? the navy? Or someone in a beret and halo with a fiery chariot parked up nearby? He dared not put his head out and see. They stopped for a moment by the candle rack but then walked on up to the altar and back down the other side. A bell rang. Maybe Saint Constance was trying to alert them to the wretched boy hiding near her perch.

Another chilly draft, and the policeman was gone, no closer to catching his fugitive but spreading the word from parish to parish, alerting people to the danger, warning them to be on their guard. . . .

One glance up at the saint's statue showed Saint Constance still dull eyed and inert, and Pepper realized that the noise of a bell had not come from her: It was the priest's doing. The door of the confessional creaked, then thudded shut. Like a café opening for business, the wooden booth was inviting customers in to confess their sins.

Pepper had not made confession for weeks. For years he had been to confession every other day. The habit had been drummed into him, like brushing his teeth or changing his pants. A boy accustomed to having his hair washed every other day would start to feel filthy after a week of leaving it dirty. So already he felt grimy in his soul, flea-hopping with sin. The habit of a lifetime hauled on him now. It hauled him onto his callused knees, and he crawled down the aisle to where the twin booths of the confessional stood side by side like coffins propped up in an undertaker's back room. He glanced back at the carved eagle on the lectern, talons spread, wooden beak quite sharp and hooked enough to tear the face off his head. If "The Hour" was near, Pepper ought to give himself a spiritual wash-and-brush-up before Heaven caught him.

Besides: He longed for someone to forgive him and say everything was all right.

The priest had entered the confessional by the left-hand door; Pepper sprinted across open ground into the right-hand booth, slamming shut the door. The priest gave a startled yelp, then collected himself and put away his library book.

"Bless me, Father, for I have sinned!"

"When were you last at confession?"

"When I was thirteen," said Pepper in his deep, gruff, fourteen-year-old voice.

Now, back in Bois-sous-Clochet, Father Ignatius—bored to distraction with the tedious little Roux boy's tedious little sins, and anxious to get back to his beehives—had trained Pepper at least to get to the point quickly. "I won't waste your time, boy, if you don't waste mine," he had in fact said.

So over the years, Pepper had rather let slip the niceties, the fancy words, the slow run-up. Now he put his mouth close to the grille and said, "Bless me, Father, for I've killed someone."

There was a sharp whistle on the other side of the lattice, as the priest sucked in sudden air through his false teeth.

"Claude Roche and maybe even the Duchess too, because he only stayed back because I wouldn't get off, and I know he wasn't there when I woke up, so I think he must be gone too. And I know I shouldn't have run, and the Lord's hand will catch up with me and grip me somewhere sooner or later. And the saints and angels are really pissed off with me because I won't go along quietly. But it was them or me, wasn't it, and they should've aimed better with the block and tackle if they were going to get me on my birthday, and not taken out Roche instead—because he's got a wife even if he is a pig. What did they want me to do? Stand still? People don't! I mean, a seagull flies over—you move, don't you? You jump out of the way, don't you? And I gave them plenty of chances afterward. And I don't see what the harm is, myself, so long as Paul's dead and gone. And he is."

There was a rapid flurry of clicks, a flicker of flame, and the smoke of a Turkish cigarette came through the grille, like a foretaste of hellfire. "You killed this Paul?"

Pepper was about to deny it, being in the confessional. Flushed and feverish, he rammed his knuckles into his mouth. He had lied in the newspaper, but it was another thing to lie to a priest. To be in this box was to be in direct hearing of the saints and angels. "Yes, Father! I killed Paul Roux! Good as. I hope so. Aunty too." Father Ignatius would have yawned by now; Pepper was rattled by the lack of yawning.

"Your aunt, too?"

"I meant, Aunty hopes—"

"Your Aunty Hope?"

It was too complicated to explain, so Pepper didn't. "Gone to Glory, that's what I put in the paper. . . . No, that was for Roche, sorry." He was not expressing himself well: He could feel it. Given a sheet of paper and a typewriter, he could have said it all easily: *L'Étoile Sud* had made him quite chatty. But there was no chief copy editor here to tidy up his jumble of words. "Now Papier's dead," said Pepper, sinking into self-pity. "And the lemurs."

"The police are close at hand, son," said the priest carefully. "You would do best to turn yourself in. If you are truly repentant, that would be the way to go."

Pepper started to make his act of contrition but broke off. "But I'm not sorry, Father! Not for running away. I don't see what else I could do. I mean, if you shoot at a rabbit, it runs away, doesn't it?"

"Rabbit?"

"Rabbit," said Pepper. "That's nature. I'm not allowed to kill myself, am I? Isn't that right?"

"Absolutely!" said the priest in a thin, high, peeping voice. "The sin of despair, that would be."

"But if a rabbit sort of actually purposely came out of its burrow and poked its head up the barrel of a shotgun, that would be pretty much like committing sui—" The thought petered out as they both, in their separate compartments, sat and pictured a rabbit with its head up a gun barrel. The problem of the ears troubled Pepper, whose thoughts were getting blurry with fatigue.

"Do you still have the shotgun with you?" asked the priest, slowly and deliberately. There was a quaver in his voice.

"Me? Oh no. I used a pistol at home," said Pepper, struck by the strange turn the conversation had taken. Father Ignatius had never wanted to talk about guns.

"I cannot absolve you of your sins unless you repent, man!" protested the priest, and so vehemently that he spat out his cigarette and banged his head as he bent down to search for it.

"Are you all right, Father?" asked Pepper.

"Repent the taking of life, at least!"

Pepper reconsidered. He *was* very sorry indeed about Roche and Duchesse being dead. And Christophe the butcher getting the wrong idea about Henri and his wife. And the ship going down. And having to lie about the lions eating Roche. And his father, possibly rotting in jail. And his mother's mortifying shame if it got into the papers . . . All this Pepper tried to put into words, for the priest's benefit, though it all came out rather muddled and left him feeling damp, shivery, and sad. So he spoke his act of contrition as the voice beyond the grille urged him to.

And then—damn it!—the priest still would not set him any penance but to go to the police and turn himself in! Father Ignatius had always given out easy, halfhearted penances, like a teacher setting homework she doesn't want to mark. *Say three Hail Marys and an Our Father and—please, boy, I keep telling you—don't come back for a week.* Not this one.

Dejected, and feeling slightly sick from the Turkish cigarette smoke, Pepper let himself out of the wooden booth, brushing down his jacket, which was dusty, creased, and torn. He knew that he would *not* go to the police and turn himself in. They would be sure to ask him his name and (unlike the priest) would check to find out if he was lying; send for his parents and Aunt Mireille. People would force his arms back into the sleeves of his former life; turn him back into Paul Roux, that boy so overdue at the undertaker's. And Mireille would snitch to the angels and saints about him, the very next time she went down on her knees. Mireille had always informed on him to the saints. *It is my sad duty to tell them what an evil boy you are,* mon pauvre.

So Pepper's sins stayed unforgiven. Once upon a time he had come out of church feeling cleaner and safer and better prepared for "The Hour." Now he just felt grubby and guilty—a fugitive still, and never able to go home.

The plaster figure of Saint Constance did not so much as turn her head to watch him go—could not be bothered to lick her cracked lips or keep safe hold of Aunty's crumpled prayer. For someone who had taken such an interest in Pepper when he was born, she seemed to have lost all curiosity now.

At least the priest would keep Pepper's secrets. That was the rule for priests: They are not allowed to repeat anything they hear during confession. And Pepper, being a stickler for rules, firmly believed that other people abided by them.

* * *

Believed it quite wrongly on this occasion.

Father André waited until he was sure the serial killer had left his church before gathering up his courage and his robes, putting on his bicycling clips, and cycling after the plainclothes policeman who had come by the church earlier. Couldn't describe the culprit (he gabbled breathlessly) not having seen his face . . . but obliged to say . . . killer roaming the neighborhood . . . armed with a pistol . . . stained in the blood of at least five victims (not counting the lemurs) . . . some of them family members . . . probably disposed of one body in the lions' den at the Marseille zoo.

The plainclothes policeman looked at him long and hard, nodding, running his eyes up and down the priestly robes, making notes but little comment. Smiling, even. He did promise to give the matter his urgent attention. Into his notebook he tucked the ten-franc note and the crumpled prayer he had picked up from the floor of the church. Evidence.

At noon—by which time Pepper was six miles away and still walking—he was overtaken by a calèche carrying chicken feed and asked for a ride.

"What happened to your hands?" asked the driver.

Pepper looked down at the puncture holes in his palms, his jacket, the thighs of his trousers, and wondered himself. Perhaps the wooden eagle had done it while he slept. Or perhaps birds of ill omen were invisible and could peck a boy to the bone without his ever even seeing them do it.

Where to hide? He had thought simply to stay out of sight of the sky and its flocks of hawkish angels. But now it seemed the police might be after him too.

"You wanna watch yourself out here," said the calèche driver. "The mosquitoes like an open wound." His gesture took in the countryside through which they were riding: marshland sudsy white with salt deposits, and the sky a great blue bowl upturned over it all. Pepper's mother (who hated having toads in her garden but was scared to pick them up) had trapped the creatures this way, on the lawn, slamming slipware cooking bowls over them and leaving them there for the gardener to deal with; china molehills that gave the occasional bump and shudder as the toads underneath panicked and jumped and concussed themselves, *les pauvres*.

"There's worse than mosquitoes, though," said the driver glumly. "They all come here to lose theirselves. The vermin."

"What, like rabbits, you mean?"

"The hyoo-man vermin," said the driver lugubriously. "Runaways. Convicts. Gypsies. Deserters. Riffraff." He must have felt he was not getting his point across, because he had a think, then added, "Ghosts."

"Ghosts?" Pepper wanted to ask whether "ghosts" included the Blessed Dead. He did not especially mind ghosts, but the Blessed Dead plucked on his nerves like harp strings.

"Freaks of nature." The driver was warming to his subject. "Goblins. All sorts. Jyoo-veniles gone to bad. There's one out there now, so the nyooz-papers say. On the run." And peering around him exaggeratedly, he brought his eyes back to rest on Pepper and to look him up and down.

"Oh, me? I'm not— Me, I've got work," said Pepper hastily. "Quite near here. In fact, if you just let me off here . . . Job on a farm. Harvesting the wheat. All that."

Again the driver looked around him at a landscape

where rice and salt were the only crops. "Best get them hands looked at, then," he said, reining in his horse.

Pepper stood in the roadway, waiting for the cart to roll out of sight. In whichever direction he looked, he could see no sign of a building, let alone a farm. Mentally he added the latest lie to his list of sins. He felt like a mountaineer adding rocks one by one to his backpack. When the cart was gone, he would go on walking: Sooner or later he must surely come to a farm. Or else, according to the signposts, he would reach Saint-Bonnard-de-la-Mer and find something, someone.

Pepper eyed the sky nervously. He felt vulnerable out there in the open, as conspicuous on the vast landscape of white salt flats and bleached grass as a beetle on a white damask tablecloth. He told himself that Pepper Roux was dead, might as well be dead, was as good as dead. Happily, there was not a rook in sight. . . .

But there were angels.

Just as anxiety and hunger took hold, Pepper was confronted by a hundred angels paddling in a lake. There was no mistaking them, lifting their flame-colored robes high to reveal spindle-thin legs. They were so beautiful, so otherworldly—sunsets made flesh, wading through their own peach-pink reflections. The cuts in his hands were infected, and he was alone and lost and afraid. What was the point in running? He did not even *want* to run from this cloud of evanescent color. He wanted to be swallowed up by it.

Unstrung by weariness, he resolved to surrender, then and there. The angel host was the color of gentleness, not wrath. So he walked toward them, while the flies blipped him in the face and the mosquitoes gorged on his palms.

What had seemed close proved to be half a mile away, but he finally picked his way to the lakeshore, over scabs of salt and knots of razor grass: "Here I am!" he called. "Look! It's me!" And he put his arms straight up in the air.

Hundreds of blush-colored shapes rose into the sky en masse.

"Here I am, look!" he called again, but they flew on: They were in flying formation, and Pepper could see that if they tried to turn back in midair, they might collide and tumble out of the sky. Once again, he had come too late and missed his moment.

SEVEN

BLOODSTOCK

When Pepper tried to retrace his steps to the road, he could not find it. So, lost, famished, and starting to panic, he was very glad indeed to come across the thoroughbred-horse breeder.

"I like horses," he said, when the thoroughbred horse breeder came out to ask what Pepper was doing on his land. "What are their names?"

"Names? They're horses. What do they want with names?" said the horse breeder.

The horses in question were brown and black but with peculiarly light manes and almost white tips on their noses. Perhaps it was a distinguishing feature of a thoroughbred horse: a pale, shaggy mane and a cream nose. The air hummed with flies.

"If you whistle, do they come to you?" asked Pepper.

"No teeth," said the man, and opened his mouth to prove it. Pepper whistled. The creatures swiveled their ears at the sound, but they did not trot over.

"Do you ride them?" asked Pepper.

"Nah," said the man. "Hernia in the unmentionables."

"Can I ride one?"

"You just try it, lag," said the man, with a snort.

There were three horses on the estate at home, but Pepper's mother had forbidden him to ride them, for fear he might fall off and break his neck. Besides, just at the moment, he could not quite see how to negotiate a path through the barbed wire.

"You good with horses, then?" asked the man flatly.

"I like them," said Pepper, hoping it sounded like the same thing. "Do you need a hand?"

For a while it seemed as if the thoroughbred breeder must have lost his ears at the same time as his teeth, because he looked Pepper up and down, turned away, and headed back indoors. "I know who you are, you know," he called, without bothering to turn back. "Read about you in the paper."

Three mosquitoes died as Pepper clenched his fists in panic.

"If you stay, you work, right? But I don't pay wages to scummy lags like you, right?" said the thoroughbred horse breeder.

"I wish I was a horse," said Pepper, standing once more at the paddock fence a week later.

A dozen brown beasts looked back at him, blinking away flies. *Can't recommend it,* said the tall one with fluffy feet.

Pepper really had found himself outdoor work, and he was delighted with it. Well, he could have done without the five-o'clock start and dragging around bales of hay that weighed as much as he did. But the customers here were so easily satisfied: They threw up their heads and whinnied as soon as they saw him.

There were horses in all four paddocks to north, south, east, and west of the thoroughbred breeder's farmhouse. Well, it was not a farmhouse exactly, but a shed built from old billboards. And they were not exactly paddocks but small patches of bald ground surrounded by rolls of barbed wire. Still, the man in the shed said that he traded in "high-class bloodstock—for the cavalry and dressage and the like." So Pepper reckoned he had stumbled into the glamorous world of jodhpurs and rosettes.

He had no idea what Monsieur Jacques had read in the newspaper—his death notice? One of Pepper Papier's articles? Or something about the sinking of *L'Ombrage?* The mystery was: How had he recognized Pepper just by looking at him—without even hearing his name? In actual fact, Monsieur Jacques never asked or used Pepper's name, but got by calling him "scum," "halfwit," "bane," "cockroach," and "lag." To a boy from a respectable home, it sounded nasty, but Pepper had gotten used to strange expressions aboard ship and tried not to mind. The horse dealer rarely spoke, but when he did, he stood still to do it, and the words fell out of him—*splat!*—so flat that Pepper could have picked them up with shovel and bucket. Monsieur Jacques was very like a horse in that respect.

Sometimes, wild horses would come roistering through the spiny, wind-crazed scrub and stand in the distance, looking at the horses corralled behind the barbed wire. They were curd white and shaggy, so their outlines blurred against the skyline, shapeless as spray. Pepper, who did not believe in ghosts, thought the cart driver must have seen these and made an understandable mistake. He whistled to them, but they never came.

"They want to meet you," Pepper told the tall horse, "but they're too shy to come closer."

I'll master my disappointment, said the horse, and lashed itself with its tail.

Pepper felt a special bond with a tall, dun cob with fluffy feet. At some time it had stumbled and fallen onto its front knees, and cankers had formed over the scarring so that the beast appeared to wear the badge of a good Catholic: devout kneecaps.

"When did *you* last go to confession?" asked Pepper.

I rarely get the opportunity to sin these days.

"Not even unclean thoughts?" asked Pepper, who had often fobbed off Father Ignatius with "unclean thoughts" when he had nothing else to confess to.

Hay, observed the cob. *I think about hay, generally. Eternity sometimes. Do you taste soap, or is it just me?*

The wild horses, curiosity satisfied, suddenly broke

into a gallop and disappeared over the horizon; they never did anything unless it was sudden. The thoroughbred bloodstock in the four paddocks all turned to face the way they had gone, and dipped their heads.

Just once, Pepper had asked the stockbreeder if he should "let the horses out for a run." The stockbreeder had said he would shoot Pepper's head off if he did, and had shown him the shotgun to prove it, so Pepper did not ask again.

There is nowhere high in the sea-fringed Camargue region of Provence: nothing much for a boy to climb. So Pepper kept a watch on the horizon and the mare's-tail clouds that streamed out on the hot, incessant wind. And he comforted himself that, by now, Aunty Mireille would be saying lots of Masses for the repose of his soul. (What did God do with those, he wondered: all those masses of Masses people recited in church? Were they like fresh straw for Him to walk on, or did they just make Heaven smell nice?)

"Do horses go to Heaven?" he asked the tall horse with fluffy feet.

Naturally, said the horse. *Who do you think pulls the fiery chariots?*

The countryside around them spread out in shadeless folds: bleached patches of land stitched together with tall reeds. The air buzzed with flies and blood-sucking mosquitoes. Pepper was glad that his seagoing jacket was also bleaching in the strong light and getting stained—he must have become much harder to spot from up above.

He did not mind at all not getting paid: He had never been paid—not even pocket money—and you can't miss what you've never had. Anyway, he loved the work. Chiefly he loved being alive.

The horse breeder's shelter was constructed like the beginnings of a house of cards—as if Jacques had intended to build up and up, a Tower of Babel made out of words:

COGNAC MONNET—*Sunshine in a Glass!*

L'OIE d'OR—Queen of Creamy Foie Gras

For Cooking, Nothing Is Better Than
VEGETALINE!

Pepper slept sandwiched between a floor that advertised:

and a ceiling that exhorted him to

BE A MAN: JOIN THE FOREIGN LEGION.

It made for the strangest dreams. Depending on whether he faced left or right, he woke looking at a green demon, brandishing a bottle of something noxious and red, or an overexcited elephant wearing a bedspread and shouting, "*I Smoke Nothing But Nile Cigarette Papers!*" (Odd—but not so cruel, Pepper supposed, as giving the elephant the tobacco to go inside them.) His bedroom was open at either end: to drafts at night and insects during the day. It did not rain once—despite the broken billboard nearby advertising Revel Umbrellas.

Jacques's den, at the heart of the structure, was more complicated to reach, surrounded by complex zigzagging corridors of plywood. At night he disappeared into it and became nothing more than a noise of snoring or the rasp of knife blades. Jacques was forever sharpening his knives.

Every third day, Jacques had a lady visitor. Unlike

Pepper, she was allowed to penetrate to the center of the house of cards. Jeanne arrived on an ancient motorbike, its panniers stuffed with bread and Dutch cheese and cheap wine, wearing a coat reinforced with strips of tire rubber, which made her resemble an armadillo. "What's *he* doing here?" she demanded as she ducked inside the shack and was confronted with Pepper.

"Lag on the run," said Jacques. "He does the horses. Leave him be."

After a bite to eat and a quarrel, Jacques would drag out a motorbike of his own from among the billboards, and the two of them would both mount up and roar away over the bumpy ground, tires skidding and skittering on slicks of marsh mud and ribs of white salt, a bucket of brown slop hanging from Jeanne's elbow. Pepper wondered if they were going to confession or to hear their banns of marriage read out in church. He was still a romantic by nature.

But then one day the bikes came wobbling back at walking pace, leading behind them, on a long rope, a horse. New bloodstock, damply brown. Pepper had to pull coils of barbed wire aside so that it could be added to the horses in the north paddock.

* * *

About a week later, Jeanne and Jacques quarreled more than usual, and some of the walls of the house of cards swayed, and the advertisement for the Foreign Legion belly flopped onto Pepper's bed. Jeanne threw a few things—knives by the sound of it; Jacques hit her and knocked her down, then crawled out into the daylight. Seeing Pepper rebuilding his annex, Jacques turned his annoyance on him.

"Don't see why you can't help me instead, useless lag!" he said, hitting Pepper with a coil of rope. And he dragged out the motorbike and told Pepper to ride behind him. Loath to cling to the man's hunched back, Pepper clung to the passenger seat instead, shut his eyes, and clenched his teeth to keep them from being shaken out of his head.

When he opened his eyes again, they were in a narrow gorge with a stream at one end. A clutter of poles had been roped together into a sort of paddock. And inside the paddock . . . two wild white horses. Alarmed by the noise of the bike, they were pressing themselves against the far fence.

"Bottle trap," said Jacques succinctly. "Push their

141

way in to get to the water. Can't get out again. Get the ropes on them, then, moron." Pepper hesitated. He had no idea how to rope a wild horse. "What you waiting for? Thought you liked the fleabags."

Pepper pushed the chest-high pole barring the narrow entrance to the pen. It swung easily away from him, then back into place; it could not be pushed open from the inside. The horses showed him the whites of their eyes. Their hooves pranced. Their heads turned a little to one side for a clearer view of him. Pepper talked to them, but without much conviction: These were wild horses, not domestic ones; maybe they spoke Basque or Romany or some Camargue dialect he did not know. "Hello, horses. Nice horses."

They threw their hooves in his face.

Pepper did not move; he only looked up. The sky over his head was an empty, blaring blue with not a bird in sight. "It's not my time," he told the horses, and they took him at his word, for almost at once they stood quiet. Jacques must have found a few teeth he had forgotten about, because he uttered a whistle of envious astonishment: The lag really did have a way with horses.

The bottle trap might look like access to water, but cruelly it stopped short of the stream. Trapped in the pen, the horses could not drink, even by stretching their necks between the poles. These two might have already stood there for forty-eight hours, taunted by the tinkling music of water, unable to slake their thirst. Pepper crawled under the end pole and cupped up water in his hands, reaching it over the fence.

"What you doing, idiot? Just get ropes on them, will you?" Jacques revved the bike.

The horses' heads collided as they competed for the water, and they knocked Pepper's hands and spilled it; he felt the wiry sharpness of their whiskers and saw the yellow shine of their teeth. He fetched more, and would have gone to and fro fifty times just to feel the soft blowing of their nostrils on his wrist, see the swiveling of their dappled ears, see up close the great blue-brown globes of their eyes with their sumptuous lashes. There was the same restless, surging energy under that white-and-cream hide as in sea waves moving under their skin of foam. It was as if two waves had broken against the shore, outrun it, and congealed into horseflesh. Their tails splashed over his head, and that touch of horsehair felt as sweet as a shower of warm rain. It was a feeling as powerful as happiness, and fear and wonder, and it rooted him to the spot. He was alive. He was feral boy. What does a feral boy want with a name?

While Pepper had the horses' attention, it was simple for Jacques to slide a loop of rope over each one's head, then turn and run. They kicked up a bit then, of course—landed a kick or two on Pepper's back as he cowered down—but Jacques was well pleased with himself, tying off the ropes to the timber fencing. He let the mares exhaust themselves, then jabbed a knife into the soft pads of their hooves, "to make them walk more ladylike," as he explained to Pepper.

At such low speed, the bike weaved and wobbled along, but the limping horses could at least keep up. Uninjured, they could have taken off at a gallop, dragging the motorbike behind them. Now, they simply slumped along, flanks brushing.

"A week from now they won't feel a thing," said Jacques. "Promise." And Pepper had no choice but to believe him.

Back at the stud farm, Jacques told Pepper to "dirty them down," and produced a can of tarlike slime and a currycomb. "It kills the lice," he said. "These beasts are martyrs to the lice."

So Pepper curried the two mares and turned them from white to the color of muddy boots. As he did so, he saw them change from white, wild horses into thoroughbred bloodstock just like all the rest: shaggy, squat, and thick-legged, drab and defeated. Flies mustered around the wounds in their feet. The rest of the horses were unsettled, pawing the ground, sawing their heads up and down, up and down. The mess on Pepper's hands smelled vile, but the taste it put in his mouth was like carbolic soap. To Pepper, everything had come to taste like soap lately. He brought the mares more water, and sure enough, as they drank, the stain washed off their noses and left them with the distinctive white muzzles all the others had.

No one paints horses brown for honest reasons. But Pepper had no way of knowing what law was being broken. People trap badgers and rats, slugs and rabbits—why not horses?

* * *

Jacques had accumulated seventeen horses.

"Enough," said Jeanne. "Let's go."

"Shift the wire, cockroach," said Jacques. And Pepper had to drag the big barbed metal coils aside while the horses in each paddock were formed into teams. Four at a time were united by a single slat of wood from a billboard, which ran under their jaws and kept them from going their separate ways (or working up to a gallop, even though their hooves had healed). They put Pepper in mind of the protesters in Marseille, united by their placards. What would horses protest about if they could? he wondered.

"Where are we going? To a horse fair?"

"Right," said Jacques. "Happy homes all around. Ladies with sidesaddles. Kiddies in jodhpurs. Big houses with stables. Easy street. Sea air and fun." *Splat, splat* went the words, and lay in the sun gathering flies.

"Thoroughbred bloodstock, that's what we got here, right?" said Jeanne, menacing Pepper with her rubber biking gloves. "Thoroughbred bloodstock bought at great expense and brought on to perfect condition. Right?"

They roped the horses into a convoy, as if, like

huskies, they might have to drag some sled. But they had only to drag their sorry carcasses over thirty miles of scrub, following behind the smelly motorbikes. Pepper rode the tall dun cob with fluffy feet. *If they tried, they could get away easy,* thought Pepper, but he knew that they would not. Perhaps they had gotten wind of the new life in store, better than the old one.

"Think. One day you might belong to someone like me," he told his mount.

Do you live on soap? said the brown horse obscurely.

The seaside town of Saint-Bonnard-de-la-Mer came into sight, first its spires, as if it were proudest of being holy, and then its factories, as if it were proud of being rich. Its curved smile it saved for its seaside visitors; approached from behind, it was a muddle of poor houses crouching down low so as not to embarrass the hilltop hotels and villas. Noon set the *étangs*, the seawater lakes, glinting like great moist eyes keeping watch over mounds of mined sea salt. Saint-Bonnard-de-la-Mer had grown rich on salt.

There was a cloud overhead in the shape of an albatross. The tide was turning, and a fine drizzle began to pepper the dusty horses—to dapple their hides. Jacques's face settled into a stupid grin, as if he were about to tell a dirty joke. "You'll want to clear off, lag," he told Pepper.

Pepper was startled. "Why would I?"

The horse breeder snorted—something he must have picked up from long acquaintance with horses.

Jeanne agreed. "You on the run and all. We know about you, see. Jacques read about you in the paper. 'Scaped off a chain gang, in't you?"

"Off a—" Pepper laughed so loudly that the horses shied and jostled. He pointed at Jacques. "I thought that was him! I thought he was the escaped prisoner!"

Jeanne laughed too, then . . . though Jacques simply reached up and pushed Pepper off the horse.

"I'm not a convict! Honest!" Pepper protested, picking himself up.

But the two drove off anyway, the jerk of the ropes almost snapping the head off one mare and making two others stumble. The dust swamped Pepper, then settled on him like sleep, along with silence as the bikes receded into the distance. He set off to walk in their wake—could no more have stopped still than if there had been a rope around his neck too. Because if he was not responsible for looking after those poor horses, then Jacques and Jeanne were right: He was nothing but a boy on the run. "Honest." *Honest*, had he said? The very word tasted like soap.

A million years before, as a little boy, he had been taught by Aunty Mireille not to tell lies. Whenever he had said (as five-year-olds do), "Look, I'm a pirate!" or "I hunted a tiger in the bushes this morning," or "There's a monster under my bed," or "I'm going to be a captain one day, like Daddy!" then Aunty had grated carbolic soap into his bedtime milk and made him drink it down, whispering, "Lies! Such a little liar! We'll have to wash the sin out of that lying mouth of yours!"

Lies (he learned) taste like soap. In the way certain smells bring pictures floating to mind, so Pepper had been left with the taste of soap in his mouth every time he spoke—or heard—a lie.

It was not difficult to follow the trail of seventeen horses, and he did not have far to follow it: Town planners don't build abattoirs—slaughterhouses—in the middle of towns but on the outskirts, where the stench can be enjoyed by the fewest people. Soon, the smell on the hot wind was so bad that Pepper gagged.

All manner of animals ended their days at the Abattoir St. Adrian: goats, sheep, cattle, and horses, though the locals tended to kill their own pigs and chickens. The law of course forbade the killing of the famous wild white horses, pride of the Camargue . . . but then the law never understood about business enterprise or canny entrepreneurs like Jeanne and Jacques. The manager of the abattoir had a nice little "backdoor" arrangement with the two of them: Jacques took a low price for the horses he delivered and, in return, the manager asked no awkward questions about where they came from. Meat's meat, and people who buy and eat it have better things to worry about than whether the meat had a name once or is protected by the law.

In point of fact, wild horses make for tough eating—sinewy in comparison with domestic horses fattened in grassy paddocks. Then again, most nags sold to the abattoir were ancient, sickly specimens that could barely drag their bones over the threshold. And wild meat has a nice dense texture that a good butcher can dress up well on the slab.

Pepper stood outside the bolted gate of the Abattoir St. Adrian and held his nose shut with finger and thumb, palm covering his mouth to keep his no-breakfast inside him. Aunty Mireille had shown him many pictures of Hell, so he could easily imagine the scene inside the gates: the meat hooks, the cleavers, the saws, the fires. . . . Just on the other side of the gate he could hear the trampling hooves of his horses—his charges—his friends—as they turned around and around in the confined space of the yard. Their whinnies, snorts, and shrieks all seemed to mention Pepper by name:

"Where's Chevalier Pepper?"

"He promised us good homes . . ."

". . . women in riding habits . . ."

". . . children in smocks . . ."

". . . meadows in flower . . ."

". . . apples in hand . . ."

". . . love in plenty . . ."

"Pepper Papier will write about us in the newspapers and make everything come out right!"

"Chevalier Pepper will free us— rely on it."

". . . as sure as the sun will come up tonight."

The gates were bolted on the inside, and very high. Pepper had been climbing things since he was four, but his hands were in a bad way, and there were no footholds at all. He stopped passersby and told them: "Horses! White horses! They're selling horses to the meat man! They're trapping horses for meat!"

No one would listen. Sleeping under a soap billboard for four weeks had done nothing to keep his clothes clean. Barbed wire and hooves had both left their marks on Pepper. The dust of the Camargue had near enough blotted out his respectability. The good people of Saint-Bonnard-de-la-Mer walked past him, through him, around him, and hurried on down the hill.

Think, Pepper. Be clever, Pepper. What do you know about gates, Pepper? How to open a gate? He thought back to the books in his father's library—remembered explosive devices lashed to castle gates—battering rams!—catapults lobbing fireballs! All he lacked was explosives or a battle engine.

He remembered how the hatch cover of *L'Ombrage* had been raised with winch and rope. All he lacked was a winch and a rope.

He thought of the power of the press, and how Pepper Papier could have written something to outrage all France and bring the police running. All he lacked was forty-eight hours and a pencil.

He thought of lobbing prayers at the sky, offering a deal, a bargain, a trade-off: *Take me instead of the horses!* All he lacked was a system of pipes that would carry his words as far as Heaven. Besides, if the angels were in need of new horse souls to draw their fiery chariots, they would ignore him.

He thought of shouting protests through the slats of the gate: *Skeleton men! Skeleton men!* But such things hadn't persuaded Captain Pepper to open his cabin door; why should they work here? So what *would* induce them to open up?

"Sell me the goat! Sell me the goat!" he shouted at the woman standing in her cottage doorway. She hastily shut the door.

Pepper jumped her gate, ran this way and that, giddy with vexation, the breath barking in his throat. He was turning into an animal, and he knew it. Animals can't think logically.

"Excuse me, madame," he said, smiling crookedly at a second woman standing in her cottage garden. "I would really *love* to buy your sheep. . . . Sorry about the clothes: I was caught in a landslide."

"Tea, dear?" said the woman.

"Thank you, but just the sheep would be nice, madame. I'd pay a good price."

"A *pastis*? You look very hot, dear."

"You are much too kind. What do sheep cost exactly? It's a very nice sheep."

"She's a good milker. Lovely cheese."

Pepper took out the contents of one pocket and held them, crumpled and bunched up, on his two hands. "Cheese too! *Mmmm*," he said appreciatively. The woman picked all the paper money out of his palms and left the prayers written on lilac paper.

Pepper knocked at the side gate of the Abattoir St. Adrian. The sheep at his knee looked up at him with yellow demonic eyes. *"I have a sheep wants killing!"* he called when he heard movement on the other side of the gate. The gate opened, but only a crack.

"Come back tonight. We got a yardful."

"I just want it jointed. For a party. Tonight." And the side gate opened a little more.

"Too much work on. Come back tomorrow, I said."

The sound of Pepper's voice had stirred the horses, like a spoon in a bowl. Their individual stamping and cribbing gave way to a shared distress. They began to circle the yard now, like water in a drain. The sheep pressed against Pepper's legs, warm and greasy, and peed on his feet, terrified by the smell of death. The slaughterhouse man scowled and looked over his shoulder at the welter of sweating, agitated horses: He was needed to quell the unrest in the yard. Pepper seized his chance. He kicked the sheep backward into the street, darted inside, and ran straight in the direction of the front gates, though his way was barred by seventeen frightened horses.

In among their legs he went, into a mangrove wilderness of moving hooves and hocks and dung and dust, ducking and threading his way through it, losing direction, jumping up to sight the gates again, barged and buffeted by the sweat-wet, brown-smeared flanks of seventeen unbroken horses. Colliding with the gates, he shot the bolts with the heels of his punctured hands, leaned all his weight against the bowing, scraping, splintery planks, and pushed.

Pepper himself spilled out into the road: A passing

pedestrian had to step over him. A mailman on a bicycle braked to avoid him. But the horses in the yard—still at last—only stared. There they stood, motionless, framed in the rectangle of the gateway.

The slaughterhouse hands, thinking the gates had come open accidentally, froze too, for fear they would spook the horses out of their trance. The situation might yet be saved, if they kept very still.

Pepper picked himself up from the ground. He stretched his arms out to either side. He snapped his fingers twice, three times. The horses swiveled their ears and turned their heads—every one—toward the boy in the roadway.

The mailman, seeing what was coming, put his feet to the pedals and shot away down the hill, narrowly missing a—"What the—?"—loose sheep. The slaughterhouse man who had opened the side gate glimpsed Pepper for the first time and bellowed:

"That b— let them out!"

The shout jolted the horses like a bolt of electricity. Legs deliberately lamed, eyes rheumy from pestering flies, sinews stringy from imprisonment suddenly recalled the wild, glittering glory of the open spaces.

So close to the edge of town, the Camargue was in plain view, beyond a garden or two. The mares from the bottle trap were first to move. They leaped from standing into a full gallop, and behind them the stained and grubby livestock Jacques and Jeanne had trapped for horsemeat turned back into the white ghosts of the Camargue.

Witnesses afterward said that the boy in their path did not move a muscle. But he did.

He tipped his head back and looked up at the sky.

Glimpsing a flicker of orange and pink above him, Pepper watched a skein of birds fly east in a flapping chevron banner of peachy splendor. After weeks working on the Camargue, he knew they were only flamingos and not an angel host. He laid no store by them as birds of omen. He just wanted to enjoy their preposterous beauty. After weeks on the Camargue, Pepper was wiser in all kinds of ways—about flamingos, about thoroughbred horses, about people.

But he still trusted horses one hundred percent.

Quite rightly on this occasion.

Witnesses said afterward that a torrent, a dam burst of horseflesh erupted through the open gates, hooves sliding on the paved roadway, necks stretched, teeth set, eyes rolling with the exertion of movement from a standing start. The boy in their path was engulfed, slight as a bulrush in a river spate. Then the horses galloped on, their wet manes shedding water drops, as whitely overwhelming as roaring surf.

And the boy was gone. All that was left was the mangled wreckage of two old motorbikes bleeding fuel onto the roadway. They turned out to belong to a couple of unsavory vagrants all too well known locally as "wrong 'uns." "Their kind—it's in the blood," people agreed, picking over the wreckage for scrap metal.

EIGHT

SWIMMER

Pepper went to the public swimming baths above the beach and found that it was easier to lose himself in a crowd than in the wide-open spaces.

He had been chased downhill by Jacques and Jeanne throwing curses at him like stones. If Jacques had brought his shotgun with him, he would have done the angels' work for them at the touch of a trigger. But unhampered by hernias or armadillo overcoats, Pepper easily outran them. At about the time the sheep found its way home, Pepper was sprinting along the seafront promenade and into the pool enclosure: a needle threading its way into a haystack.

The pool was set into a concrete pontoon: a rectangle

of seawater and litter. Algae on the walls had turned the water bottle green. Pepper sat and caught his breath. The noisy splashing nearby brought back to him the day he had picnicked on a riverbank at home, watching other children playing in the water while he sat sandwiched between two women discussing suitable hymns for his funeral.

There were children playing here, in the emerald-green pool—jumping in, diving, splashing, floating: children much younger than Pepper. He wished he had defied his mother—taken a risk and plunged in. He wished he were one of those children now—five, seven, nine years old. He wished he could take over the life of one of these children and be allowed to swim, to be young again—not have to inhabit an adult's life anymore, with all its bewildering complications and unkindnesses. He even walked along the edge of the pool, looking at the many piles of clothes strewn about there. What if he were to put on those dungarees, those short jackets, those small shoes . . . would they make him little again? Their smallness made him huge—one of the Ugly Stepsisters wondering how to fit her great hoof into Cinderella's tiny slipper. The children in the pool shrieked, plunged, bobbed, laughed, and slithered in and out of one another's shiny, wet arms. But Pepper was marooned on the desert island of fourteen, cut off from being little ever again. He had no choice but to be a man. The tears brimmed over and ran down—which was appalling in someone who is supposed to be being a man. Birthdays ought to be optional. Then he could have stopped at thirteen and stayed thirteen forever, at home with Mama and Papa and Aunty.

Pepper lay down on the cracked concrete terrace, his jacket rolled up under his head.

"You should go in, you should," said a youth in an undershirt and shorts, sitting down beside him. He was a swarthy, skinny chap no taller than Pepper, though old enough to have attempted a mustache. The top of his head was sunburned and peeling, so he looked like a baby with cradle cap. "Healthy, that water is. Heals all sorts."

Pepper looked doubtfully at the cigarette packets and dead wasps floating in the water.

"You should go in, you should," insisted the stranger. He had a double-headed eagle tattooed at the top of one of his skinny, muscular, sunburned arms.

"I can't swim."

The youth barely blinked. "Betcha can in there. It's the salt. Keeps you up. Trust me. You look like a swimmer. I'll look after your things."

So Pepper took off his shirt, trousers, socks, and shoes, and he eased his way, gawky and nervous, down the pool ladder. Its rungs were slimy with seaweed. The saltwater stung the holes in his hands. Looking down into deep water, he thought for a second he could see Roche submerged and beckoning. . . . But it was only a deck chair that had blown into the pool the month before, canvas billowing in the green depths.

In comparison with hot, white daylight, the green water was very cold. But the idea of getting clean persuaded Pepper down the ladder. His reaching toes found no bottom—the pool was deep. He did not let go of the ladder, having learned recently not to trust everything he was told—but he was pleased to overcome his fright. *Come on, then. Drown me,* he thought, and let go of the ladder.

He sank like a stone. Luckily the ladder came to hand again, and he hauled himself back into the air, coughing and gasping.

Just as he got into the pool, everybody else started to get out. Pepper thought it must have something to do with the film of filth spreading out like an aura around his body, but in fact it was just the weather's doing. Locals recognized the ominous signs: black clouds rolling in to snuff out the sun, gusts of wind scuffing the water's surface, the deck chairs shiftily shuffling this way and that. By the time Pepper had begun to enjoy himself, holding on to the ladder by just one finger, floating, treading water, changing hands, he was alone in the long green pool. The sea's grumbling had grown to a roar. When the rain began, he did climb out— harder going up, harder because he had not eaten today—and ran back toward the warmth of his clothes.

Except that his clothes were gone.

So was the stranger with the eagle tattoo.

Pepper looked this way and that, scoured all the spots where his clothes might have been put for safe-keeping—and found nothing. He climbed a wall to look along the beach, to try to spot the stranger, and all the time a snicker in his throat was growing into a giggle and then a laugh, then a big, uncontrollable fit of hilarity. Finally he had to stand and lean his hands on his knees and laugh and laugh and laugh. Someone had stolen Pepper's outside! For weeks he had been trying to run out of his skin, only to be fleeced of it by a stranger.

The rain came down on him so hard that his skin roughened and turned blue. He was shuddering violently with cold, but there was no one there to see. It was as if the entire population of Saint-Bonnard-de-la-Mer were made of sugar and had melted away.

A line of laundry, pegged out to dry in a garden, hung so heavy with rain that the shirt and trouser cuffs were dragging on the ground. Pepper unpegged his new identity—a man's, of course; there were no boys' clothes available—and tried to put it on. Surprisingly hard to slide cold wet arms into cold wet sleeves, cold wet feet into cold wet trousers. The overlong legs folded under his feet, so the lack of shoes hardly mattered. He set off to walk, feeling in every pocket for a clue as to his name or what he now was, this flapping, shivering, undersized Jonah swallowed by his clothes. Nothing.

His muscles began to work of their own accord,

contracting, knotting, stiffening; they pulled his head down toward his chest and made him hunchbacked. He could not shed his shroud of an outfit, because his fingers were lost inside the cuffs and rigid with cold.

Oddly, it got warmer after the sun went down. Well, intermittently warm and cold, as though sea waves were breaking over him on a sunny day. And then, by turns, hot and icy, as though winds off the Sahara and the Russian steppe were taking turns to blow on him. After the rain stopped, the clothes did dry on him, except around his feet. Scuffing through mud and grit had crammed his trouser cuffs, so they swung with every step and each caught the other ankle and tripped him. On and on he stumbled, past shops and garages, houses and a hospital. If he saw someone coming, he turned left to avoid them. Or right. How vast the town must have grown, that he walked for hour after hour and never reached its edge. Out of the corner of his eye, he saw herds of horses stampede out of alleyways, and all the streetlamps wore haloes—their gas flames watched him with grinning, sneering faces. Saints lurked on basement steps, or under hatches in the pavement. The pavements under his feet

165

lifted and rucked like a hall carpet in a draft.

One by one, the town gave up its sinister nighttime secrets. When, on hands and knees, he looked down through the metal bars of the drain covers, he was sure he could see prisoners manacled there. The cats of Saint-Bonnard-de-la-Mer were long-haired patches of darkness, prowling the roofs until they spotted a boy and came down to sink their long teeth into his cold, flapping hands. The statues discussed him, calling him "cockroach," "lag," and "bane."

A gendarme looked into his face and asked him his name and where he lived—questions far too hard for Pepper to answer, given the pain in his chest. Luckily a commotion in the next street drew the policeman away and left Pepper in peace, sitting with his back to a shop window. Opposite was another sheet of glass—an aquarium?—and within it the most terrifying vision of all. Floating there, white gown spreading out and clouds of white light veiling his head, eyes fixed steadfastly on Pepper, was the pale form of an angel drowning.

Pepper curled himself up into a ball, keeled onto his side, and made himself so small that the rainwater gushing down the gutter had no difficulty in washing him entirely away.

* * *

Circles expanded to the size of planets and shrank back to pinpoints. Fish hatched out of the pinpoints and grew and grew until breath bubbled from their mouths, and from the bubbles more fish hatched, and more and more and more, and they all had to be organized, slotted together . . . except that Pepper was a thousand miles out in space and his arms were a thousand miles long. He was separated, alone, drifting, and nauseous, tumbling through darkness. . . .

So it was nice waking up in the hospital. The sheets were so smooth, he could not feel his body. The pillow was so soft that he might have been afloat. The smells and sounds were so strange and uninvited that he knew they had nothing to do with him. He did not have to do anything about anything.

Ever again.

He had finally outrun his body.

For there he was in the next bed! His clothes hung at the next-door bed-curtain rail, like a man cut down from the gallows: his bleached, braidless navy jacket, his nicked and torn trousers. His body made a mound under the next-door blankets. Pepper squinted down:

Yes, there were his sensible lace-up shoes, scuffed, colorless, stained by the sheep. No clothes hung at the end of his own bed. Ah well. Ghosts don't need clothes.

But apparently they do need to cough. Suddenly a string of coughs ripped through Pepper like a gas explosion demolishing a house. Around the room, a row of heads lifted and watched him with more joy than he thought was called for. "He's back with us, nurse!" called one old man. Even Pepper Roux in the next bed sat up and looked across as well as he could with two black and swollen eyes.

Except that it was not Pepper at all but the stranger from the swimming baths—the one who had stolen his clothes.

"Five parts dead and gone you were when they brought you in," said the thief, as if he were bringing Pepper up-to-date on a football score. "Bad night to sleep out in the rain. What were you drinking?"

Pepper did not trouble to answer. Words had to be mined from somewhere too deep inside him, and though he could feel them, like lumps of coal in his chest, he could not muster the energy to fetch them to the surface. With immense effort, he lifted one hand

and waved it in the direction of the thief.

"Me? What happened to me? Yeah! Right! What happened to me? You want to know what happened to me? Common assault, that's what. Aggravated bodily! What am I doing? I'm doing nothing! Who am I harming? No one! Then along comes her. One minute she's got her arms around me, and I'm thinking, *Do I know you*, right? *Get off me; I got standards.* Next she's punching seven colors of the rainbow out of me! And you know what? (You don't, trust me.) She never even robbed me—well I'd got nothin', but she couldn't know that, could she? Woman scorned, right? Woman scorned, that's what I reckon. I was too slow—I'm guessing now, right? I'm too slow with the *romance*, and—*wham!*—she's all set to kill me! But I mean fair's fair: You're not expecting that kind of thing from her kind, are you? I mean women are women, yes; there's no telling with women. But a *nun*?" This lament was addressed to the ward at large, and the other patients shook their heads or tut-tutted or got on with reading their newspaper, having heard it all many times already. The words rattled down on Pepper like a million horseshoe nails: too hard and sharp, too bent out of shape to be useful. And he dreamed that horses were galloping to and fro over him, trampling him into deep, soft leaf litter—painlessly, painlessly—to hide him from flocks of rook-black nuns on motorbikes.

Pepper could not fathom, at first, why the thief did not apologize, or even mention the pool and the matter of the stolen clothes. But the fact was, Pepper—washed, brushed, soothed, and smoothed, hands bandaged, body tucked into a hospital bed—looked nothing like the gullible boy on the beach, the one so easily persuaded to leave his clothes in the care of a stranger. Konstantin Kruppe simply did not recognize him. Besides, addicted as he was to taking other people's belongings, Kruppe tended to look at people's pockets and not their faces.

Konstantin would slip out of bed at night and help himself to things from the drug cabinet at the end of the ward. He did it not so much to dull the pain, or to get better, or to alter his brain waves, but just to prove that he could. The drug cabinet was kept locked, and Konstantin bet the other patients he could get it open in under a minute. No lie—he could. Tablets, syrups, powders, capsules: He tried them all.

As Pepper began to recover—and he did so amazingly fast on three square meals a day—he watched with a kind of fascination as Konstantin helped himself to another patient's tobacco, drank ethyl alcohol from the sterilizing bowls, sniffed oxygen from a cylinder in the corner. . . . It was not so much the desire to have it as the getting something for free. Konstantin's unhappy experience with the violent nun had wounded his masculine pride; it was as if he had to prove he was a hard man and a true master of his trade, even if that trade was thieving.

In the depths of one dark night, Pepper could not contain his curiosity, and asked, "Konstantin— are you that man who escaped from a chain gang?" Konstantin (who was just then standing astride Pepper so as to unhook and steal his bed-curtains) looked down at him sharply. "We wrote about you in my newspaper," said Pepper.

"No fooling! You did?" And Konstantin beamed with pleasure to think that his name had appeared in the papers. "You tell anyone, I'll have to kill you," he added, and Pepper nodded.

"Is it safe to stay here?" asked Pepper, who had been

considering staying for as long as possible. "The food's good."

Konstantin wrinkled his nose, so his front teeth showed, mouselike, under his little mustache. "Nah. I'll be out of here tomorrow. Get a bike. Always a bike rack outside a hospital. Bike around to Nice or Cannes. Kidnap a millionaire. Nice fat ransom. Something along those lines. Want a candy?" and he pulled out a fistful of pills filched from the drugs cabinet. "I like the red ones."

Pepper politely turned him down, so Konstantin swallowed the whole fistful himself.

Next day, the police arrived to arrest Konstantin. But he had made good his escape once and for all. The stolen jacket and trousers were still hanging there at the end of Konstantin's bed, but Konstantin had cunningly eluded his pursuers. The bed sheet was pulled high up over his head, and its soft, white folds softened out the spiky shape of his dead body.

"Sudden death," said the nurse, seeing the shock on Pepper's face. "These things happen. No reason. Patient seems to be making a good recovery, then . . ."

She snapped her fingers. "Gone."

Pepper was not taken in: He could see her hands shaking and the way she fretfully bit her lip. He had half a mind to explain what had happened and put her out of her ignorance. Because he knew very well why Konstantin Kruppe was dead: There was the suit of clothes that had done him in.

That murderous nun who had attacked him in the street: that must have been Saint Constance, making her saintly rounds, scouring the streets for a runaway fourteen-year-old. Recognizing Pepper's clothes, thinking it was he, she had tried to wrest him away to Heaven. Foiled by the ambulance service, doctors, and nurses, she had sent assassin angels to the city hospital, and they too had seen the clothes and made the same mistake. They had sucked the breath from the wrong set of nostrils, snatched away the wrong soul.

So close! They had come so close! Pepper's mended hands clutched the pillow so tight that the soft white cotton tore.

Head nurses, doctors, and police murmured together in the corridor. There was someone else out there—a monumental shape in white, palely looming beyond the glass door, wanting access to the ward. But the police, smug about catching up with Kruppe, were treating the place as their own, denying entry. It was probably only a doctor, but Pepper saw angels in every flicker of light, every splash of white. He slipped out of bed, took down the coat hanger, dressed in his familiar scruffy shirt, jacket, trousers, shoes. Finding the wads of lilac prayers still crumpled at the bottom of the jacket pockets, he even stopped to write on one: *Rest in peace.* And left it on Konstantin's chest.

They say that God moves in mysterious ways, but Pepper had seen quite enough to know that God's saints and angels couldn't organize a duck hunt in a shooting gallery. Yet again they had taken aim at Pepper, missed, and flattened the wrong duck. He was not about to let them get their eye in and hit the target.

NINE

GOOD NEWS BOY

There is always a bicycle rack outside a hospital. Pepper chose the smallest bike parked there and rode away. For two days he cycled, feeding himself on sunflower seeds plucked from flowers as big as dinner plates that grew alongside the road. The sunflowers looked back at him blankly, taller by a head than he was, their crispy ripe faces bent downward as if in sadness or shame. Perhaps they were ashamed of having nothing better to offer him: Sunflower seeds are not very filling.

Pepper himself was not terribly ashamed. After stealing a ship, it did not seem so terrible a crime to help himself to sunflower seeds, or even a bike. A bike equips a person to make himself useful—to be a telegram boy, for instance. Pepper, you see, had come up with a plan. He would cycle until he reached a sizeable town, then enlist as a telegram boy.

There is no such thing as a telegram man or telegram woman. Only boys will do. As he cycled, the years fell away and he was thirteen again, free of the burden of being doomed, en route to a career delivering good news to kindly people. He had had so many names that he wrote "K.K." on the cuff of his shirt, to remind him of who he was now. As soon as he reached Aigues Mortes, he searched out the offices of the Postal and Telegraphic Services of France and offered his services.

"Name?"

"Konstantin Kruppe, sir."

"Do you know the area, Kruppe?" asked the head of telegrams. "You need a sound knowledge of every street to do this job."

"Of course!" groaned Pepper, who could suddenly see the glaring snag in his plan. It had not occurred to him before.

Luckily, the telegram supervisor misunderstood *of*

course and took it to mean that "of course" Pepper knew the city as well as the creases in his own bike saddle. He gave Pepper a round peaked cap and an armband and assigned him a stool to sit on in the outer office. "You are working for tips, you understand? Not a wage."

"Of course," said Pepper, undismayed.

He was glad to see there were two other boys already sitting there, clasping their caps on their knees. With luck, the office was so overstaffed there would be no work for Pepper to do: He needed time to think.

"You'll be Zee," said one, looking him over.

"All right," said Pepper, who liked to oblige.

"I'm Exe. He's Why. The Kaiser in there"—he nodded toward the Telegraph Office—"he's working his way through the alphabet. He can't remember names. What's your real name?"

"Konstantin Kruppe."

"In that case, you're better off with Zee," said Why.

"What happens after me?" inquired Pepper, having been assigned the last letter of the alphabet.

Why shrugged. "He goes back to the beginning, I s'pose."

Exe nudged Pepper. "Or maybe you're the end of the line." And they laughed, but not unkindly.

Within five minutes Exe was dispatched to rue des Amandiers with a telegram. Within ten, Why had been sent to the Hôtel St-Georges with another. Pepper looked out of the window, noticing how enormous the town had grown since he'd last looked: Every district a web of streets, every street a row of buildings, every building a clutch of separate lives. How could a boy from out of town even begin to—

"Here, Zee. Here's one for the Lost Luggage Office!" called the supervisor of telegrams.

Pepper gave a whoop of joy. The Lost Luggage Office had to be at the railway station! And there were street signs to the station! With the tip he was given there, Pepper would buy himself a map of the city, study it all night, and by tomorrow be as ready as anyone to dart around Aigues Mortes delivering good news. He closed his eyes and slipped the cap onto his head—remembering, remembering—folding his ears forward but finding no need; the cap fit perfectly. *Go ye into all the world,* the Bible said, *and spread the good news.* Pepper had every intention of being the best telegram boy in the south.

178

Following the signs for the railway station, Pepper rode into the center of town for the very first time—a town so beautiful, so astonishingly old, that he lost his way a dozen times just staring around him. Cobbles jolted loud shouts of pain out of him, and huge walls barred his way, so he had to keep retracing his route. When he finally found his destination, the man in Lost Luggage gave him a lecture about riding a cycle on railway property.

Pepper stood there, waiting for his tip, looking around him at the treasure trove of things left behind by careless train passengers. Baskets, coats, books, parcels, and umbrellas, of course, but a stuffed bird, too, and an accordion. There were three suitcases in three different sizes—as though they belonged to the Three Bears. Perched on a high shelf, like Papa Bear, Mama Bear, Baby Bear, each case had initials embossed into its brown hide: AAB, GGB, EPB. He wondered where the family had been going, how they had all three lost their luggage, and what bears kept in their suitcases. There were also a car wheel and a crutch; a shotgun, a wheelbarrow, a hookah. What kind of people had owned these things, and how were they feeling now that they had lost them? Or how would it feel to own such things but leave them all behind one day in jumping down from a train, going on your way empty-handed, free . . . ?

"No reply, I said!" snapped the man in Lost Luggage, and dismissed Pepper with a flick of his hand.

No tip?

No tip meant no map!

Pepper sat astride his bicycle, head sunk between his shoulders, and took off his cap. He knew nothing of this city, its labyrinth of streets, walls, and towers. Too late in the day to bother going back to the Telegraph Office—besides, without a map he was unfit to serve. He was finished as a telegram boy.

Women at windows plucked the curtains shut. The alleyways filled up with dark. Flames flared up in the faces of strangers as they passed, lighting cigarettes. All the old fears mustered, just out of sight, weaving nets out of the darkness, bunching the nets in their hands ready to throw over him.

On the other side of the street, the doorway of the Hôtel du Gare was a golden glow, its windows a column of golden dashes rising into the sky. Pepper had the old, overwhelming desire to get up high and check for approaching danger. He went inside, walked directly to the elevator, and rode up to the roof.

Lights, stationary and moving, reflected or flickering, greeted him as he stood on the parapet and looked out over the city. Somewhere an ambulance bell sounded. A handful of vehicles moved along the distant highway. The ancient city walls formed a black arc devoid of light. The sea was the end of the world. Pepper checked the sky for flaming chariots and found it hysterical with stars. He checked the streets below for saints patrolling. Any one of the glimmering cigarette tips, the cone headlights, might be someone searching. . . .

Pepper wondered if it was possible to die of loneliness, and if that was why God had divided Himself into three—Father, Son, and Holy Ghost: for want of companionship.

On his way out of the hotel, between the elevator and the revolving doors, he passed a rack of leaflets and maps. A detailed street map of Aigues Mortes showed him every street.

"Please, may I take this?" he asked the receptionist.

"Take anything you like," she said without even looking up. "Everyone else does."

Night after night, Pepper studied the map, memorizing the street names, famous landmarks, shortcuts. In the early morning he rode the same streets for two hours at a stretch, noting the culs-de-sac, the worst hills, the most excruciating cobblestones: learning his trade. Then he reported in to the Telegraph Office and joined Exe and Why on the three stools in the outer office. They talked to him; they liked him. And then there were the dogs. . . .

Almost everywhere he called with a telegram, his knock was answered by hysterical barking. Pepper approved. Dogs are what he would have spent his money on, if he'd had any. He liked dogs—liked the whole idea of dogs—and dogs seemed to know it, because they never barked at him for long. Of course, that probably had something to do with the biscuits. And the biscuits had something to do with why he still had no money. Now he spent his tips on biscuits, which he fed to the dogs until their tails wagged.

Exe and Why hated dogs—were always getting nipped or chased when they delivered telegrams. So Pepper bought *them* biscuits, too, and explained the whole biscuit/wag ratio. They were so grateful that they said he could sleep at their place, a loft on the rue de la Poste. Outside the tiny fanlight windows, starlings filled up the gutters each evening, like running water. They skittered across the roof tiles on their tiny claws; their clamor was louder than the church bells.

"We could buy a dog between us!" suggested Pepper, looking around him delightedly at his new home.

Exe and Why could not see the appeal. "We're not made of money," they said. And Pepper certainly had none left after buying dog biscuits for three.

But it was wonderful. He delivered telegrams of congratulations to wedding feasts, where they made him join in the dancing and plied him with wedding cake. He delivered word of jobs won and exams passed.

"I have a granddaughter!" said the woman on the rue Carrefour, and kissed him and gave him ginger ale. A man who had inherited ten thousand francs even gave him ten francs and told him not to gamble it away.

Mièle Rosette, who had an odd sort of boarding-house on the place des Marins, got regular telegrams. She took them from Pepper and thrust them away into her bosom without a glance while, with the other hand, she loosened his tie or ruffled his hair. Seeing the "K.K." on his shirt cuff, she asked what it stood for. It seemed absurd to say that it stood for "Zee."

"Konstantin Kruppe, madame."

"Oooh! That's a big name for a little man," she purred, and sprayed him on the ear with a little bottle of perfume she was holding. Sometimes she answered the door in her dressing gown, and once—not. For years Pepper had been innocently confessing in church to "unclean thoughts," and doing penance for them, without ever knowing what they were. He reckoned he had a credit now on the unclean thoughts front—enough to cover him for a few sightings of Mièle Rosette in her negligée.

Of course, there was the old man whose telegram told him his wife had died in a sanatorium far away in Switzerland. "I can't remember her face," he said to Pepper. "Can you remember?" And Pepper had helped him search the bureau—"Can you remember what my

Renée looked like?"—until they found a photograph of the wife.

And there was that lady who screamed. . . .

The franc she had tipped him was still in his hand as he reached the bottom steps of her apartment. Then the scream came. Looking up, he saw a window smash and the woman's hand emerge, shards of glass glittering high overhead, slitting the light into colors: a shattered rainbow. When he got back to the Telegraph Office, Why had pointed out two sharp shards still stuck in the shoulders of Pepper's jacket.

"She'll have lost someone in Africa," said Why, the voice of experience. "Lots of deaths right now. Had two this morning. Hate delivering those ones."

"Sometimes they even thump you. Like it's your fault," said Exe, nodding gloomily. "Who'd join the Legion when there's a war on?"

"Who'd join the Legion?" said Why.

Pepper looked down at his palm and saw that the one-franc tip had made a round, black bruise in his tightly closed fist. Like a bullet hole.

So after that, Pepper—or Zee, as the boys in caps called him—opened all the telegrams before he reached the delivery address. He found that when the yellow envelope was too well sealed, he could wet it in a puddle and it came open easily. If the news was good—a baby, a marriage, friends visiting—he delivered it with a smile and a salute, and in the sure and certain hope of a tip. If it was news of a death, a prison sentence, a bankruptcy, then Zee . . . well, Zee *obeyed his conscience.*

Tragedy was not what he had pictured as he cycled between the sunflowers with a high heart and an empty stomach. His calling had been to make people happy. Perhaps the escaped convict Kruppe, in wearing Pepper's jacket for a night, had stained it with more than his sweat, blood, and hair oil. *Take what you want:* That had been Konstantin's religion. Now Pepper was infected with that same ruthless desire to have what he wanted. And he wanted people to be happy.

"My bike skidded, and I was in the canal before I knew!" said Pepper to Madame Falconnier.

"You poor boy," said Madame F. "Sit down. Take off that wet coat. You'll catch your death."

Pepper assured her that the accident did not matter at all—except it had made him lose the telegram he was bringing her. "Scooped it out . . . came apart . . . like wet bread . . . nothing left . . . ," he explained sorrowfully. He had had time to read some of the words, though, and would she forgive him?

Madame F. sat down, hands pinned between her knees to stop them shaking. "Something terrible's happened, hasn't it?" she said at last. "My boy. My Marius. Something's happened to him."

"No!" Pepper hastened to tell her. *"No, of course not!"* Her son Marius had quit the Foreign Legion after he had become nearsighted and couldn't hit the target anymore during rifle practice. (A shame, because he had just been promoted to captain for bravery.) Hearing tell of Brazil, he had decided to go there with friends and pan for gold until he had enough to buy a ranch in Argentina. Or Patagonia possibly. He might be gone a long time. Ten years. More. But she was not to worry, because somewhere her Marius was getting fat on roast beef and riding beautiful horses over the pampas. Praying for her every night before bed.

"I think they have the same saints in Brazil. They'll deliver prayers between you. On Sundays. Maybe." Pepper added this personal footnote to the lost telegram. There were all kinds of other details he had wanted to add but thought it best not to. After all, how much could one telegram plausibly have said? Wishful thinking would fill in the gaps. In the future, Marius's mother would look up at the moon, and it would be the same moon that shone on her distant, daring son. And for her there would always be the possibility that one day the adventurer would come home, riding up the street—a Patagonian caballero in leather chaps, silver bolo tie, and solid-gold spurs.

Deep in Pepper's pocket, in among the lilac prayers, stained by no one's tears but his own, lay the undelivered telegram. Interfering with official mail was a heinous crime—but not so bad (Pepper thought) as telling a mother by telegram that her boy has been shot for cowardice and buried in the desert sand. Even in Pepper's own skull, those words slopped about like molten lead.

"Are you *crazed*!" shrieked Why. "That's tampering, that is! They can get you for tampering!" Pepper only shrugged. He had more fearful enemies than the French telegraphic service.

Now when he dreamed, the saints came after him wearing post office uniforms, telling him to report at once to Hell. He tried to run, but his pockets were too full of lies. So they covered his head with a hood and stood him against a wall and took aim on his heart. . . .

But by day, Pepper delivered happiness, spreading good news—nothing but good news—as far and wide as his stolen bicycle would carry him.

He did not deliver, to the girl whose sweetheart had jilted her, the telegram that read:

MET SOMEONE STOP

DO NOT LOVE YOU NO MORE STOP

LEAVE ME BE STOP

He told her instead that her fiancé had joined the Foreign Legion and been killed in Africa, her name on his lips.

He told the man whose telegram read:

EMPLOYMENT HEREBY TERMINATED STOP

189

that the Hongriot-Pleuviez Amendment had forced the company out of business, but they wished him well in his future career and thanked him for his hard work.

A young singer called Chantal dreamed of studying opera at the Conservatoire de Musique in Paris, so her hopes would have been dashed by the callous words

```
REGRET APPLICATION UNSUCCESSFUL
STOP
```

Instead, Pepper told her that the principal conductor had fallen madly in love with her during her audition and, being a married man and a good Catholic, dared not invite her to work nearby him day after day, for fear of temptation.

"But he was almost fifty!" exclaimed the girl. "Almost dead!"

"Not dead to love," said Pepper sternly.

One man telegraphed his wife to say he had found an apartment to rent but that dogs were not allowed. She was to have Beowulf put down. Pepper told her— nothing at all. He simply sneaked the dog out of the garden and home to the loft on the rue de la Poste.

190

"Just for a while," he told Exe and Why, slipping the wolfhound another biscuit. "I'll take him back soon." Though that just added one more lie to all the rest.

Of course, his job took Pepper to the garden gate of other people's lives without ever quite letting him inside. Every day he saw children playing in gardens, smelled cooking or heard quarrels through open windows; saw women heaving shopping bags in at front doors, kissing sons good-bye for the day with packed lunches. He saw fathers come home and pull out bunches of keys—*Hello, dear! I'm home! How are the children?*

And Pepper's heart yearned toward those doorways like a dog on a leash, and he would have to haul it back, speak sharply to it, tame it, before stepping back onto the pedals of his bicycle and setting off to spread a bit more joy.

Anyway, he had a home now too, high up, with a view over rooftops to the sea. He made himself a bed out of a postal sack stuffed with shredded undeliverable mail. Each evening the starlings roared over Aigues Mortes—he could hear them clear through the roof, see them mobbing one another outside the tiny eaves window. As the sea light faded, the birds' twittering merged into a single high-pitched whistling note—a curfew siren warning the city to light its lamps. For half an hour, the sharp rooflines were softened by the wavering movement of a thousand thousand birds roosting for the night. Were the angels as countless as this, Pepper wondered? Were they as small? He had always pictured them big, like albatrosses or golden eagles, but perhaps they were little, like starlings—or smaller still, so that they could ride the starlings over the darkening streets: pilots on reconnaissance missions.

From the loft window, Pepper had a clear view of the city's tallest building—the Constance Tower—impaling the sky on its blunt tip. The starlings that massed each evening did not exactly rain down destruction on the town, but they did loose a lot of guano: It clung like cake icing to windowsills and public monuments. The Constance Tower suffered worst of all, and scaffolding caged it now while the guano was cleaned off. Still, the statue of the woman that stood on its summit rose above such indignities. She had the perfect vantage point—could surely see everything and everyone in the city. So he never stood long at the window, watching the starlings.

"If anyone comes asking, please don't tell her I'm here," he said to Exe and Why, who looked at each other in alarm.

One day, a telegram took him to the rue Méjeunet. He wondered why the name was familiar. Was it from his nightly studies of the map? He was sure he had never cycled along it before.

Iron or wooden gates—once splendid—led off the road into hidden courtyards strewn with litter. And on three sides of each courtyard there rose up high, shabby apartment buildings. The crying of babies intertwined into a continuous wail, like distant wolves. There was a smell of drains, pigeons, sorrow. Bellpulls had been ripped out, leaving only stalks of rusty wire. There were no numbers on the doors: a mailman's nightmare. He would have to ask around for number nineteen.

A tarnished courtyard fountain featured a cherub spewing water. Pepper propped his bike against it, but the bike fell over. Children with dirty faces squatted down and set the back wheel spinning.

"Mind your fingers," said Pepper. Laundry draped over ropes high above dripped on his head like tears. He took out the telegram to check the name.

Like the bike wheel, the buildings around him suddenly began to spin. His mouth turned dry as dust. His legs would not carry him. He bent to drink from the fountain. Hidden by the rim—Pepper didn't see it until he ducked his head to the spout—was a dead sparrow. Waterlogged little body, claws curled tight shut.

It was Roche under 2,600 fathoms of ocean.

In snatching his head away, Pepper scraped his forehead. Damping his fingers in the drinking fountain, he opened the telegram:

```
WE REGRET TO INFORM . . . BELIEVED

   DROWNED . . . SS L'OMBRAGE

      FOUNDERED. . . .
```

Then he wadded the slip of paper into a tiny yellow pellet, thrust it deep into his pocket, and pedaled home at breakneck speed.

He was no sooner through the door than Exe and

Why grabbed him by the lapels and pushed him backward onto the landing—"Go! Get out of here!" Pepper leaned against their rigid arms, resisting. Inside, Beowulf began barking. Starlings stood on the far side of the little eaves window and watched expectantly, tapping the glass with their beaks. The latch hung off the door, the wood around it splintered.

"Someone came looking!" said Why, the fear still in his face.

"A priest," said Exe.

"Some priest!" said Why. "Customs officer undercover, more like!"

They had just gotten home from work. A knock at the door. Being a week behind with the rent and having an illicit dog on the premises, they did not answer. Exe looked through a crack in the wood. Beowulf began to bark and growl, but the priest outside barked louder.

"Pepper? You got Pepper in there?" he demanded, and a boot slammed against the door, smashing the lock. The priest burst in and searched the bathroom, alcove, boxes, shut the dog in a cupboard, overturned the beds, screamed after them as they fled down the stairs, *Where is he?*

"We didn't dare come back till he was gone. *Now* look!" said Why, and relented enough to let Pepper see the wreckage for himself.

"'Pepper'?" said Pepper. "Are you sure?"

"'Pepper,'" said Why. "That's drugs, right? Gangster talk for drugs, right? Something you put up your nose. We told him no one lived here but us." But the two drew back from him, severing acquaintance. They did not wish to see him killed by any evangelical priests or arrested by Customs, but Zee had taken one step too far into the world of crime, and they no longer wanted him for a friend.

"No wonder you told us not to open the door!" they called after him down the stairwell, their voices full of disappointment and hurt feelings.

"Crazed," said Exe, turning back into the loft. "Told you he was."

"Crazed . . . ," Why agreed. "Do you think we can keep the dog?"

"Where's number nineteen?" Pepper asked the children in the courtyard off rue Méjeunet, but they were too young for numbers. "Number nineteen?" he called up at an open window, and a man leaned out and pointed. The cracked and stained stone staircase had long since lost its handrail, but that helped, since Pepper was carrying his bike as he climbed. He knocked on a door scabrous with peeling paint. After a long wait, a woman opened it as far as the chain would allow.

Yvette Roche's skin was the color of damp salt. Even her brown hair, unbrushed and shineless, was salt streaked, her lips bloodless. The permanent frown between her blank, bleak eyes was the shape of a rook. At some time in the past, her nose had been broken.

For a while, they looked at each other: the woman, the boy. Seeing his cap and armband, she grudgingly took the chain off the door. Deep in his pocket, Pepper fingered the tiny ball of wadded-up telegram. Stepping past her into the hall, he took off the cap and hung it on a coat hook.

"Hello, dear. I'm home," he said. "How are the children?"

TEN

THE GOOD HUSBAND OF AIGUES MORTES

There were no children, luckily. Pepper was relieved. He quite liked children, but not as much as dogs.

Do people see what they expect? Or do they see what they choose? Yvette Roche said nothing about her husband's unexpected return. Or how much he had changed. But then Yvette Roche said nothing anyway. She never spoke. Her bruise-colored eyes followed Pepper warily around the apartment as he hung up his jacket, washed the dishes, poured himself a glass of water, browsed through the cupboards for something to eat. At least when he took out the trash, carrying two large bags of it downstairs to the courtyard bins, she did not lock the door on him.

True, she was not so wifely that she hurried to serve him scrambled eggs with grated cheese on top or pour him a rum, but then there was no food or drink in the whole apartment. Pepper could see he would have to stop buying dog biscuits and start buying food instead.

It seemed a bit of an imposition to be there, getting in the way. (Aunt Mireille had always said what a nuisance men were around the house.) But he knew it was his responsibility to provide for his wife, to put food on the table. Now that he was Claude Roche.

He could not go back to the Telegraph Office—clearly the saints were onto him—so Pepper got himself a job as a grocer's delivery boy instead. Gaspar the grocer took no interest in him, beyond his name—"Claude Roche, sir!"—and how little he would cost.

"If your work is satisfactory after one week, I may employ you." That was the deal.

Every day Gaspar laid out a row of shopping lists on the back counter and, taking each one in turn, Pepper would assemble his deliveries. Fetching the items from the shelves—soap, coffee, rice, cheese—he packed a large flat-bottomed basket, then lashed it to the front of his bike and wobbled his way around to the customer. The customers liked him, liked his good manners and the little extra errands he ran for them: walking their dogs, mailing their letters, pumping up their tires, finding their spectacles. They paid their grocery bills cheerfully enough—though not to Pepper; Gaspar would never have trusted a grocery boy to handle money.

Gaspar alone did not pay his debts. One week's probation turned into two, and still there was no mention of wages. Pepper did not mind. He had already adapted—as endangered animals do—to his new habitat. The last basket of the day he filled with things for Yvette Roche—pâté, coffee, eggs, cakes, honey, bread—and cycled home with them balanced on the front fork of his little bike, gradually stocking the kitchen cupboard with things he remembered seeing at home.

Still Yvette said nothing—though she was quick enough to eat the food, working her way backward through any meal: coffee, dessert, salad, pepper salami. . . . He watched her eat—covertly at first, but then quite openly, knowing she would never look up while there was food on her plate. Her skin was a grimy gray, her eyelids flaky; and her red lips peeled and bled where she constantly bit them. And when she was not eating, she could sit perfectly stock-still—as birds do when a cat is passing by. Only when his back was turned did Pepper sometimes feel her eyes resting on him; when he turned back, she would start eating again—quickly, eagerly, as if harpies might swoop in at the window and snatch the food away. Meanwhile, Pepper kept up the kind of conversation he thought married people ought to be having: "The price of fish is up again." "Honestly, the traffic these days!" Pepper Papier would have turned every sentence into a question. Pepper Roche never did, because he knew he would not get an answer.

At night Pepper curled up on the split and sagging sofa, and its broken springs drove nightmares into him through spine, hips, and head. Yvette Roche was as gauzy thin and silent as a suit of clothes hanging from a hospital coat hanger. But Claude Roche, who haunted his dreams, was solid as a side of bacon, as real as a punch or a kick. He hunted Pepper through the bilges of the sunken *Ombrage*, through schools of drowned sparrows. Pepper gasped for breath, woke up with his lips tight pursed against drowning. The dreams were as real as real as real. By comparison, Yvette Roche was shadowy: a noise in the next room, a perfume on the stairs. Pepper found himself wondering whether she was really there or had died before he arrived and left only her ghost eating meals from back to front.

Her flaking lips put Pepper in mind of the statue in the Church of Saint Constance. Throughout his childhood, the saints and Aunty had watched over him like prison warders, but now that he had escaped, he rather missed their tyranny. So without knowing it, he began to bring things to Yvette like oblations to the feet of a holy statue—honey and cheese, lentils and wildflowers, scallions and artichoke hearts. He brought her herbs that sounded like incense: turmeric, sassafras, coriander, oregano. . . . They filled the apartment with strange scents—sharp, sweet, experimental. Yvette experimented with cooking them. One day, she set in front of him a plate of pasta. It was seeded with pine nuts and vanilla pods, stranded with cress and egg, anchovies and honey, and it tasted like—nothing he had ever eaten before.

"Mmm! That was delicious! Thank you," he said, putting down his spoon (there were no knives or forks, only spoons). Yvette herself was eating honey, holding the jar in her lap, out of sight, taking quick, furtive sips off the tip of a spoon. All the pasta was on Pepper's plate. Only when he pushed the plate away from him did she reach out a finger and surreptitiously ease it within reach, spooning up what was left. He wanted to ask: Is there only one plate? He wanted to ask how she could eat cold pasta. But Yvette's wrapper of silence was like a dead man's shroud: He would have been scared to look inside.

He wanted to ask why she had opened the door, why she had let him in, why she had believed . . . But each day these unspoken questions just had to curl up a bit tighter and make room for fresh ones. *Lie still,* he told them. *I am Claude Roche. She believes me, look. I am Claude Roche. I used to be a real pig, but people can change, can't they? I am Claude Roche now.*

He dreamed that a telegram came from the angels:

```
PIG DUE AT ABATTOIR STOP PORK BEST
WHEN PIG IS YOUNG STOP AM SENDING
        CHRISTOPHE THE BUTCHER
```

Pepper woke screaming. A hand was in his hair! *Christophe's hand!*

But it was only Yvette, standing stiffly beside the sofa, stroking his hair from arm's length, making a soothing, shushing sound that sank in an instant to silence. Seeing him free of his nightmare, she turned and went back into her room.

The neighbors heard the screaming and thought it was Yvette. Claude Roche must be home from the sea again, the pig: He always gave his wife cause to scream when he was home between voyages. They shook their heads and wondered why God had not done the decent thing and drowned the man long since. They did not go to Yvette's aid, exactly, but they did what they could. They snitched to the landlord.

So, soon after that, the landlord came beating on the door. Yvette stood in the bedroom doorway, clutching closed her dressing gown, biting her lip white. A voice bellowed: "Three months behind with the rent, Roche! Heard you were home, Roche! Cough up or get out. Last warning! You got till the end of the week!"

Claude Roche had run up all kinds of debts and left them all to his wife when he died. Now it was Pepper's job to pay them off, to take over his debts. After all, he had taken over the rest of the man's life. That evening, by way of an apology, he brought home five coconut cakes, each with a glacé cherry on top, like the flame on a white wax candle.

"Tomorrow I'll ask him for pay," he said emphatically. "I will."

Yvette Roche wiped the cream off her nose and nodded. "Yes. You should do that," she said. It was the first thing she had ever said to him.

The cakes, though, were a mistake. It so happened that coconut cakes were a particular passion with the grocer. Gaspar resented parting with them to customers—he often ignored them on grocery orders. When he had to sell one, he felt like a man who has had his pockets picked; he kept track of the exact number left on the shelf, looked forward to taking them home for his supper. So when five Holy Candle cakes disappeared at the end of the day, all sweetness went out of his nature, too. He was waiting for Pepper the next day, hands on hips, a grim smirk of satisfaction clenched between decaying teeth.

"Thieving little lifter," he said. "They transport boys like you to the swamps of Australia. Feed 'em to crocodiles. I'm calling the police." Power tasted almost as sweet to Gaspar as coconut cream.

But he should have waited for Pepper to dismount. As it was, the thief sank all his weight on the bike pedal and sped away, shouting over his shoulder, "Take it out of my wages, cheapskate!"

Pepper was not unduly worried about losing his wageless job. But for the first time ever, he felt the need of money. Wives were not like dogs; they could not get by on biscuits. He needed pay.

He tried at the town theater first. If there was one skill he had mastered, it was changing roles, and he thought that fitted him very well for acting. But the theater manager looked at him for two seconds and said, "Go home, lad. You're a child. What are you—fourteen?" and turned him out of the theater.

Pepper had to return to the glare of sunshine outside, where people either squinted at him, one eye closed in suspicion, or never bothered to look at him at all. He walked down to the sea, but none of the fishermen at the *poste des pêcheurs* needed a deckhand. He asked at the department store, but his clothes were now so shabby, they disguised any skill Pepper might have with slicing machines or pneumatic cash systems.

And as he roamed the city looking for work, a familiar feeling settled on him like snow: the feeling of being watched. He could no more throw it off than he could slough off his own shadow. He glanced toward the Constance Tower, with its woman on the roof—just to be sure she was still up there, in her right and proper place. It was just the idea of her, wasn't it, that prickled the back of his neck? He began to run—could not help himself—down the steep stone steps, between the tightly packed houses, across the canals by way of the narrowest bridges.

He experimented with being someone else—someone more like Konstantin Kruppe or Roche. After all, Yvette had married him, so she must like that kind of man. He practiced swaggering; he oiled his hair flat against his head, smoked cigarettes, and whistled at a woman in the next street. It had an effect, but not quite the one he was after.

"No. I don't like him," said Yvette Roche, tugging the cigarette out of his mouth and throwing it away before lapsing back into silence.

He experimented with wearing Roche's clothes, too, exchanging his own bleached, torn, and shabby jacket for cotton shirts that flapped around his small frame like slack sails around a mast. There was a white sailor's hat, too, grimy with hair grease but jaunty.

Of course, this did mean that when he went out, Yvette was able, for the first time, to go to the peg in the hall, take down the small, braidless naval jacket, and go through the pockets.

She found the prayers, as creased as fallen lilac leaves. She found the letter "Captain Roux" had begun long before, in pencil, aboard *L'Ombrage*.

> Dear Madame Roche,
>
> I am very sorry ~~in deed~~ indeed to tell you the sad news, but your poor ~~husbund~~ husband Monsieur Roche is dead. I did not ~~no~~ know him very well, but I expect you did. I am sure he is happy with the saints.
>
> Your ~~obediant~~ obedient ~~servent~~ servant . . .

She found several yellow pellets of wadded-up paper, devoted an hour to picking them undone and flattening them out on the table. Finally she found the one addressed to herself. Informing her of the death of Claude Roche.

When Pepper came home, she served him a supper of croissants stuffed with peas and honey, which they ate with their fingers because she had sold all the spoons. She had sold the crockery, too. Luckily, they did not need plates: The dining-room table had been scrubbed so clean that it was three shades lighter. And while they ate, Yvette Roche said . . . nothing at all.

Rumor spread beyond the apartment buiding that Roche was back in town.

Pepper had been down to the docks, looking for work on the boats without success. But as he walked home, he was busy thinking about something else: about the big woman with the baby carriage. He had seen her first near the bullring. He had seen her again at the garage, had seen her at the church where he went to make confession. Her carriage, anyway. He was sure it was the same carriage because one of the wheels was buckled and didn't touch the ground. At the church, he had gone over to the carriage—in the same way he went up to dogs tied up outside shops—glanced inside.

No baby. Strange.

Pepper's fruitless search for work had taken him in all

directions, and yet the baby-carriage woman had steered the exact same course. He glanced behind him as he turned the corner into the rue Méjeunet: no sign of her, thank goodness. And when he turned back . . . there was the carriage, parked outside the vacant apartment building on the opposite side of the road. Pepper glanced instinctively toward the Constance Tower. That was why he collided with the three men at the foot of his stairs.

"Is this him? This is not him. I saw him once. This is not him," said the first.

"Who are you?" said the second.

"Claude Roche," said Pepper agreeably.

"Been ill, must have," said the third. "You been ill?"

"I was in the hospital for a while," said Pepper.

"Told you. Said he'd been sick."

"Going to be sicker now," said the first, and punched Pepper in the head. He reeled from the surprise as much as the blow. "Heard you were back. Big Sal heard. Big Sal wants the eight hundred and fifty francs you owe." And he punched Pepper again in the chest. Then, finding their range (they had been expecting a much bigger man), they continued to punch Pepper in the stomach and kidneys until he fell to the ground.

Then they kicked him—unexcitedly, routinely—as if to say, *Nothing personal, but business is business.*

Neighbors gathered at the top of the stairs, intrigued. Yvette came out and threw a saucepan down the stairwell, and the attackers decided to leave. Pausing to retie his shoelaces, one leaned close to Pepper's ear. "Don't play poker if you can't afford to lose," he remarked, and parked his chewing gum on Pepper's forehead.

They had seen the naval cap, heard the right name, seen the person they wanted to see: Pepper could not blame them for beating him up. He had set out to fill the place of Claude Roche, and from what he knew, Roche probably deserved it.

"So how much did he . . . How much did I . . . How much do we owe? In debts," he asked Yvette as she dabbed at his face with a washcloth.

And the woman laughed—a hollow, horrible laugh. Her arms spread wide, limp at the twig-thin wrists, like broken wings. She looked for a moment like Roche awash in the hold of *L'Ombrage.* She said nothing, but that gesture said it all. Gambling debts, fines, rent, loans: Roche had sunk her a thousand fathoms deep in debts—then left her to drown alone beneath them.

That night Pepper dreamed that Roche was in Heaven, wearing the standard-issue wings and that malevolent grimace of his. He swooped down, brass bucket hooks for claws, his white gown glowing red with the reflection of fire. "Why are you in Heaven?" Pepper asked, and Roche replied, "'Cause you took my place in Hell, Skeleton Man."

Pepper reviewed what he knew about earning money quickly and easily.

What would his father have done? Sunk a ship.

What would Roche have done? Stolen something, pawned something, sold something that did not belong to him. No! No, Roche would have made a bet and then made sure of winning it.

So Pepper insured his life: *L'Ombrage* had taught him all about insurance. There were premiums to pay, of course, but within days he had the necessary francs. After all, life had taught him a thing or two.

What had his time in Jacques's billboard shack taught him? That elephants smoke Nile cigarette papers, and that real men join the Foreign Legion.

ELEVEN
LEGION

"What's your name?"

"Roche, sir," said Pepper.

The sergeant scowled. He had known a man called Roche once, in Nantes. "Knew *of* him, leastways. Claude Roche. Killed a friend of mine. First name?"

"Legion," said Pepper wisely.

The sergeant put down his pen. "Are you trying to be funny?"

"'My name is Legion: for we are many,'" said Pepper.

"What?"

"It's from the Bible."

"It's from the Bible, *sir*!"

"It's from the Bible, sir!" But Sergeant Fléau, who (it

was said) could bayonet men with his insults, was at a loss for words. As a small boy he had learned, from the back of his mother's hand, never to hit anyone with the Bible. He wrote out a form for Legion Roche—did not even quibble when the boy refused to give his home address: Recruits commonly did.

What he saw when he looked at Pepper's earnest little fourteen-year-old face was anyone's guess. But he needed his quota. Operations in the Sahara were going badly. For every yellow telegram sent home after a death, a replacement soldier had to be recruited and shipped out to Africa. What the sergeant needed was names on forms. Besides, the boy could shoot straight—which was more than any of the others could: the immigrant builder, the laborer without identification papers, the unlicensed smelter, the Gypsy salt shoveler.

While Pepper signed the forms, all these others were having second thoughts. The night before, up at Le Petit Caporal bar, over the hairdresser's shop Cheval Cheveux in the rue de la Ravette, it had seemed like a good idea. If they could stick it for two years, they would earn French citizenship. After a few free drinks, they had all been feeling patriotically French. As patriotic as skunks, to be honest. Now that they had sobered up, the lure of adventure had waned.

Arriving at the recruitment office next day, seeing Pepper sitting in the recruiting line, each in turn had laughed. But when the boy proved to shoot better than they did, they had decided he might bring them luck. Little Legion could be their mascot. Being religious—well, he could quote from the Bible, couldn't he?—made Legion even luckier, just as a holy medal is luckier than a rabbit's foot.

From Pepper's point of view, the Foreign Legion was ideal. Men who enlisted were never, ever asked about their backgrounds, where they lived, or why they wanted to join up. Criminals and illegal immigrants, bigamists and debtors joined the Foreign Legion to lose their pasts. Quite often they lost their lives, too, but what with the insurance policy and his overdue appointment with death, that suited Pepper very well.

Twenty or so recruits turned up and were enlisted. To assess their merits as soldiers, and to pass the time while they waited for the next naval transport ship, Sergeant Fléau took them all out onto the salt flats. The weather obliged with African heat and a plague of sand flies. He made them run a mile, rifles held over their heads. He had them down on hands and knees, polishing one another's boots. He had them standing to attention in the full sun until one by one they fainted. And all the time he promised worse to come in Africa. Mustafa, Norbert, Albert, and Nadir cursed and howled and looked to Pepper to make himself useful and die before they did, so that Fléau would have to relent. But Pepper did not weaken. Aunt Mireille (when Mother wasn't looking) had frequently subjected Pepper to just this kind of pastime, telling him, "Better to suffer in this life than the next." He was an old hand at torment. No, Pepper endured the sergeant's games with patience and goodwill.

He was looking ahead to Africa. He was looking, in fact, even farther ahead than that—to the life insurance check Yvette would receive when he died in Africa. Pepper was looking ahead as far as Hell itself, and the fact that he would have to go there unless he could pay off Roche's debts—his sins and his IOUs— before the saints and angels caught up with him. True, he was in pain a lot of the time and frequently wished he were dead. But at night his dreams had become so fearful that he no longer dared to sleep. The sergeant seemed soothing by comparison: His threats did not disturb Pepper. It was simply a shame the sergeant felt the need to shout.

"What I don't understand is why he doesn't just ask nicely," Pepper would say as they bedded down among the thistles. And then Mustafa, Norbert, Albert, and Nadir would stop cursing Fate and roll around laughing instead.

Things didn't begin to go wrong for Pepper until they got on to bayonet practice. The sergeant set up a dummy stuffed with straw, and the new recruits were encouraged to charge it, bayonets fixed, and to stab it enthusiastically with a ripping motion. It was not a very realistic dummy; it didn't even have a head. But there was something reproachful in the way it bled straw from its guts after Pepper bayoneted it. For the first time, a nagging doubt edged into Pepper's head. His plan to be a telegram boy had almost failed for want of a map; now he was starting to think that, in joining the Foreign Legion, he had overlooked a major snag.

He had done well with a handgun, because the target had been an inanimate object. At home he had shot empty rum bottles off gateposts with his father's pistol. But not rabbits or deer. Not even the rooks. Never anything living. "Will we have to . . . I mean . . . I suppose in Africa . . . ." But even he could see that the question was too stupid to ask, and he stopped short of asking it.

"Enough of the baby games!" bellowed the sergeant. "Your enemy don't sit around waiting for yuh! Moving targets!" And he actually smacked his lips at the prospect of his idiot recruits' failing miserably to hit a moving target. A picture formed in Pepper's head of Claude Roche coming for him, coming at him, running at full tilt. His gun was almost a comfort.

But the moving target Sergeant Fléau had in mind was not. It was absolutely not.

A troupe of wild white horses had just materialized out of the sun's glare: clouds forming over a mountainside, spray breaking over rocks. The recruits fumbled halfheartedly at their cartridge belts.

"Head or heart. That's the only thing that'll bring 'em down," said the sergeant. "Aim at the head or heart."

The horses looked. The recruits looked back. Not a rifle was raised.

218

"They're not moving, sir," said Norbert.

"They will when you start shooting."

"They're protected, sir," said Pepper.

"So's the Empire, lad," said the sergeant. "And we're the poor sods who have to protect it. So make the first shot count, 'cause you won't get a second chance where you're going."

"Do they come at you on horses in Africa, sir?" asked Albert.

"Are you trying to be clever, soldier?"

Go! thought Pepper. *Run!* He thought it so hard that the thought solidified in his brain, hard and round as a bullet. *Go!* he thought, words exploding in his head, aiming the thought at head and heart of the horses. His tongue curled into the shape of a trigger. *GO!*

Quite suddenly, the white horses turned and melted out of sight. The legionnaires breathed out as one. The sergeant swore.

Then he marched them, double-time, through the heat of noon, to the shore of a salt étang. The lake was aswarm with flamingos.

"When I stir 'em up, you fetch 'em down," said the sergeant. "I want one dead for each and every one of you, or you'll be sorry your mothers ever bore you. In fact, you'll be sorry your grandmothers ever met your grandfathers." And away he went, muttering the kind of threats he thought might encourage them.

"At least there are plenty of them," said Albert, taking out his teeth and putting them in his shirt pocket: The rifles did kick.

Already some of the others were taking aim, wanting to be ready as soon as the sergeant scared the birds into the air. Horses had felt wrong—they had balked at horses. But looked at the right way, these were birds, just birds. And there were so many that it would be hard to fire and not hit at least one of them, despite the glare.

The whole scene wavered in the heat, unreal, insubstantial. Mirages filled the landscape with pools of nonexistent water. Groups of flamingos glided in various directions, to and fro, currents within currents, hundreds within thousands, as beautiful as any sunset.

Thou shalt not kill. Pepper wondered how he had ever overlooked such a big drawback. Hell-bent on getting killed, he had overlooked the other aspect of life in the Legion: You had to kill people. In Africa it would be people, not horses or flamingos. Pepper reached an important conclusion. He was not a man after all. He could no more shoot someone than fly.

Sergeant Fléau, keeping well clear of the firing line, raised his pistol. The recruits tried to make sense of their safety catches. Over the horizon, where thick haze swallowed the nearby highway, a small dot appeared—a noise no louder than a fly buzzing. The shape grew to the size of a lump of sugar, a die. The sun flashed on a car's windshield. Irritably, Fléau lowered his gun. Now he would have to wait for the car to pass. Strictly speaking, it was probably not legal to use flamingos for target practice.

In the heat-warped landscape, the vehicle appeared to float high off the road—to approach through mid-air, humming. Spellbound, the recruits watched as it took on more solid shape: shining bumper, smiling grille. When it was on a level with them, it turned off the road and came bumping over the grass, caked in dust. The driver's door opened a crack as he cruised past the line of recruits.

"Taxi for Roux?"

Pepper fell to his knees. The chariot had finally swung low to carry him away, and just in time to prevent him going to Africa and killing people.

Unhesitatingly he got in.

The sergeant was stretched up to his full height now, like a meerkat, trying to see, through the distorting haze, what was happening back among his recruits, why the car had stopped, who was undermining his authority. As the taxi pulled away, he started to run back. The car backfired.

The flamingos on the lake rose up—a volcanic upheaval of red and pink. Most of the trainees were staring after the taxi, slack jawed, but a few, already scared into blind obedience, heard the bang and opened up on the flamingos as the birds flew overhead showering down water drops and guano.

One bird landed dead on the roof of the taxi, wedged on the roof rack, its long, rosy neck snaking limply down behind, so its beak tap-tapped and its feathery cheek smeared to and fro across the rear window. Pepper put his arms over his head, drew his knees up to his chest, and slid into the gap between front and back seats. As the car jolted its way back to the highway, the driver's seat back pounded him in the face like a debt collector.

* * *

It was not a long ride to Heaven, and most of it was on the flat. When the engine died, and Pepper finally plucked up courage to look up, the driver—who must have been a North African, cocooned entirely inside a black hooded kaftan—was hunched over the steering wheel. "Here you is," he wheezed.

It was rue Méjeunet, and at the top of the cracked, concrete stairs Yvette Roche was waiting with a meal of scrambled eggs topped with grated cheese. The apartment had bizarrely broken out in Christmas, because Yvette had found herself work assembling tree decorations: fifteen centimes apiece. Baubles, stars, and fairies. Angels. After supper, they sat opposite each other, slotting the wings onto angels.

"Did you send the taxi?" he asked.

"Taxi?" she said.

They should have talked more. Yvette, at thirty-five, had a wider general knowledge than Pepper. For instance, she could have told him that deserting from the Foreign Legion is punishable by firing squad.

Then again, if he had known, Pepper would only have worried. And life was too short for worry. Pepper's life, anyway.

TWELVE

BIG SAL

You could say Beowulf the dog was to blame. But maybe it was the singer who started it.

Chantal, the would-be opera singer, threw a brick through the window of the telegraph office. "That telegraph boy lied!" she warbled, and threw another brick.

Those few simple words—*the telegraph boy lied*—were enough for the telegraph supervisor to invite her in, sit her on a stool in the front office, and hear her out: how the telegraph boy had told her she had been rejected by the Paris Conservatoire only because the maestro was in love with her. His lie had cost her a trip to Paris and humiliation at the hands of an aging maestro, who had thrown her out on her ear.

"So he must have invented the message and not fished it out of the canal at all!" Chantal concluded.

The supervisor was appalled. He did not care much for opera, but, to him, tampering with the official mail was high treason. He pointed to Exe and Why, but Chantal said that neither was the boy who had lied to her. So it had to be Zee.

Luckily, the supervisor had no memory for names. "Zee. *Zee!*" he yelled, snapping his fingers at Exe and Why. "What was his real name?"

Exe and Why looked at Chantal and the bricks on the floor. They recalled their roommate, the various ways he had turned bad news into good. Exe shrugged. Why shook his head. They could not remember Zee's real name, they said. Chantal went away unsatisfied. Justice was not done.

So it *was* Beowulf's fault, really.

Next day, Why was cycling past the shop of Gaspar the grocer when he thought of trash cans. Life in the loft apartment had come to revolve around Beowulf the dog. He and Exe had discovered just how deeply a hound can sink its teeth into a boy's affections. They adored the beast—made it their life's work to put food in Beowulf's ever-empty stomach. So, seeing Gaspar's trash cans, Why stopped to look and found, to his delight, a ham bone carved down to its gristle, three stale baguettes, some slimy brisket, and a broken jar of morello cherries. He was just loading these into a vegetable crate when Gaspar grabbed him from behind and propelled him into the outhouse, jamming the door shut.

"Got you! Got you! Got you!" he bawled childishly through the rotten wood door. The next time Why heard voices, Gaspar was excitedly telling a police officer, "I knew it was him straight off—by the hat! He worked for me a while back—stole from me!"

Why, who had spent an hour eating morello cherries and watching maggots crawl over a rank hambone, was in no mood to be arrested for something he had not done. Gaspar, who never looked at faces, thought Why was the boy who had robbed him, but Why was having none of it. "You mean Zee, that's who you mean. His name's Konstantin Kruppe, if you want to know, and he *used* to do telegrams, but he *doesn't now!*" And Why thrust his armband in the grocer's face.

By the time they all got to the police station, the crime had shrunk, rather. On paper, the theft of five coconut-cream cakes did not look like a hanging offense. But the name *Konstantin Kruppe* was faintly familiar to the desk sergeant. His eye drifted to the wall of peeling wanted posters.

WANTED
KONSTANTIN KRUPPE
(aged 19 years)
Escaped felon.
REWARD PAYABLE
for information leading to recapture.

Such notices are never updated: They accumulate. Prisoners are caught, join the Foreign Legion, escape the country—maybe even die in hospital beds in some nearby town. But the misleading wanted notice stays on the police station wall for years after.

"This Kruppe character—he's a menace, you know," he told Why. "Escaped from a chain gang. String of convictions. You know him by sight. If any of you telegram boys spot him in the street—"

"Telegraph *operatives*," said Why, pointing to his armband.

"There's a reward," said the sergeant.

And there it was. A month before, chain gang or no chain gang, "pepper" or no "pepper," they would not have delivered up their ex-friend to the law for love or hard cash. But Beowulf cost a fortune to feed. They had responsibilities. So the idea of a reward had them cycling the streets in the early morning and after work at night, scouring those parts of the city where a criminal on the run might turn up. They studied every face they passed on the pavement, hoping for a glimpse of Konstantin Kruppe. They wanted that reward. If they found him, it would be the end of the line for Zee.

Meanwhile, Pepper and Yvette Roche filled their apartment so full of Christmas decorations that children from up and down the rue Méjeunet came to see. Pepper (who liked to make people happy) drew the curtains shut, lit candles, and called it a "magic grotto." He told the children stories—first the ones he remembered from his father's library but then ones of his own inventing. They tasted rather soapy—stories are only lies with a plot, after all—but he could not see the harm. He told them of sea monsters and pirate treasure, of rainbow-colored lemurs who stole from trash cans, and of fiery flying chariots—adventures so exciting that the little girls squealed and shivered and chewed one anothers' braids.

Unfortunately, these happy children were not a paying audience, and all the Christmas baubles, when they were finally packed and delivered, paid just 237 francs.

"Maybe Big Sal will let us pay in installments," said Yvette doubtfully.

"But this money's for the rent!" Pepper was shocked. He was sure there were more important debts to pay off before Roche's gambling debts.

"If we don't pay the rent, the landlord will only send in the bailiffs," said Yvette. "If we don't pay Big Sal, he'll send those men again to beat in your head. Anyway. . . ." She seemed to be of two minds about whether to go on. "Anyway, I paid the rent already. That's to say, a friend of mine did. Paid the rent."

Pepper was even more astonished. Yvette had changed, true, since her dead husband's homecoming: Her skin was clearer, her hair shiny and combed. Her lips no longer flaked (except when she was eating croissants, like now), and she was not so thin. She even smiled sometimes—even spoke and went outdoors. But he had never realized she had *friends*. Suddenly he remembered all those romances in his father's library. "Oh!" he exclaimed delightedly. "Do you have a lover, then?"

The croissant exploded. Peas skittered across the table. Yvette coughed. The cough became a laugh—a high, bright, sunny, ringing laugh the like of which Pepper had never heard before. Not even at home in Bois-sous-Clochet. "And me a married woman? *La!*" she said, sweeping peas and crumbs into a pile with the sides of both hands, trying to make a serious face.

Pepper was disappointed. He knew he was ignorant for fourteen—being kept home from school and everything—but a lover would have been a big help to Yvette. After Pepper was dead.

He put on the cap and shirt that made him feel most like Claude Roche and pocketed the 237 francs. "I'll take this to Big Sal now. In case I don't come back, I think you ought to know: I have life insurance." Saying it made him feel older, less of a green boy.

After he had gone, Yvette searched his belongings again and found the life insurance. She did not laugh at finding it. In fact, for quite a long time she stood at the window and cried.

* * *

Big Sal ran a gambling den in a cellar under the Cheval Cheveux hairdressers in the rue de la Ravette. He sat at the bar now, underneath the coil of the cellar steps, beside his moll, a blonde who was busy opening new packs of playing cards with her long red fingernails. Big Sal was unimpressed by the boy in the sailor's cap and overlarge shirt.

"Where's Roche?" he said.

"I'm Roche," said Pepper, and laid the money down on the mirror-tiled bar.

"Didn't know he had a son."

"He doesn't. I'm Claude Roche."

"Well, you've got noive. Coming here. Seeing what you done to my boys."

The protester in Pepper protested: "What? Did I graze their shoes with my face?"

"And paying me back with dough you took off my own collectors? Funny man, ain't yuh!"

"*I* took—?"

It was Little America. Everyone at Big Sal's spoke with an American accent—spoke French, but with an American accent. Pepper, who had never met an American, thought they must have their mouths full of food.

Big Sal's bartender rounded the end of the bar, making a noise with his cocktail shaker like an angry rattlesnake. "Yuh flattened 'em, that's what yuh did. Yuh flattened 'em. With a baby carriage."

The lights overhead flickered ominously.

Pepper could not imagine who had flattened Big Sal's thugs. But he picked up his envelope off the bar again: He would sooner pay the next month's rent with his hard-earned francs; the landlord at least swore in a proper French accent. The envelope was spattered with water drops—perhaps the cocktail shaker was leaking.

Big Sal snapped his fingers. The bouncer climbed the stairs to lock the street door. The light socket fizzed.

"What's he doing here, Sal baby?" asked Sal's moll. She was wearing sunglasses, which meant she could not see the cards or very much of what was occurring.

The bouncer was in a tussle with a newcomer at the door—"Let me in, you fool!"—and the resident stripper pushed past him, muffled up (despite the heat) in a full-length fur coat. "What's going on?"

"Just getting set to kill someone," said the bartender.

Pepper looked upward, thinking there could be no birds of ill omen in a basement. But there it was, sure enough: a raven-shaped stain spreading darkly across the ceiling. Big Sal snatched the envelope out of Pepper's hand and looked inside.

"Well, look at that. The guy's here to gamble! Right? Can't stay away! Am I right?"

"Addict," said Sal's moll, chewing. "Should I deal the cards, Sal honey?"

"I only know pairs," said Pepper, not liking the way things were going. He fixed his thoughts on the life insurance and determined to see things through to the bitterest of ends. On the whole he would have preferred to be assassinated by angels. At least they operated above ground and probably spoke French without American accents.

Big Sal was amused, intrigued, possibly even drunk. He pushed a pack of cards into Pepper's hand and watched him deal them facedown on the bar. "I don't know this one," said Sal's moll. "How come he don't play poker, this guy?"

"There's another good reason to kill him," said the bouncer.

"How d'you play it?" asked the bartender.

"K.K.! It's little K.K., isn't it!" exclaimed Mièle

Rosette, slipping out of her fur coat and knocking off Pepper's cap so as to ruffle his hair. "What's my little K.K. doing here, Sal?"

"You know this guy?"

"Sure! He's a telegram boy! Konstance Krunch or some mouthful the like of that."

"Says he's Claude Roche."

"That pig? No way. He's long gone."

The staff of Big Sal's were slow to pick up the rules of pairs, they being more used to blackjack and poker. But soon they were all gathered around the bar—waiters, a bouncer, a pianist, a moll, and the cloakroom girl—picking out two cards at a time, cursing or congratulating themselves.

"Tell you what," said Big Sal, flapping Pepper's money. "I'll just call this a fine for what you did to my boys."

Clouds of red mustered behind Pepper's eyes. "I didn't do a thing to your 'boys.' Yvette and I earned that making Christmas decorations!"

"Ah! Sweet!" mewed Sal's moll sentimentally. "I love Christmas!"

"I heard Claude Roche was dead," said Mièle Rosette loudly and clearly.

"I got a pair!" said the bartender.

"He hit my boys with a baby carriage," said Sal, slapping down his palm in the middle of the bar, scattering the cards. "Kill him anyway."

Then the lights went out.

Water began to gush down through the ceiling roses, along the wires and onto the bulbs, causing short-circuiting. In the darkness, the sound of rushing water was terrifying. Bottles of liquor and the glass lights behind the bar fell with a crash. The playing cards washed off the bar. Pepper felt something brush against him, slick as a wet otter, as Mièle swept her coat up out of the wet. "Get out of here, kid. You got friends waiting," she said in an undertone so soft, he thought he had imagined it.

Pepper felt his way toward the stairs as more and more stalactites of water streamed down the wiring, cold and startling in the dark. So close to the sea, it was easy to imagine that the tide had somehow overreached itself, was pouring into the cellar, and would quickly fill it to the brim. So the others too were making for the only exit, competing for use of the stairs that wound up and over the bar, toward the street door. So

Pepper climbed up the *outside* of the banister.

Not for nothing did Big Sal hold sway over the gambling underworld of Aigues Mortes. He knew it was not the sea pouring into his swanky premises. "I'll kill those bastards upstairs!" he raged, groping his way instead toward the bar takings and the jacket with his wallet in it. A lump of plaster fell from the ceiling and caught him between the shoulder blades.

"I locked it! It's locked! Just wait, will you!" said the bouncer, fumbling at the padlock, but someone jostled him in the dark, and he dropped the key. Water and lamplight were pouring now through the gaping hole in the ceiling: Street lighting was one thing the hairdressing salon enjoyed that the basement nightclub didn't. The bouncer barged against the door with one shoulder but bounced back, lost his balance, and fell down the stairs, dislodging the bartender and a flurry of curses. Leaning out from the banister as far as possible, Pepper felt around with one foot for the surface of the bar and lowered himself onto it. Big Sal, on hands and knees, was feeling his way up the stairs, crawling over his fallen staff members. When he reached street level, there was a bang and a flash as he fired a gun at the padlock. Only then did he look back and see the shape of little Claude Roche, arms stretched upward, rising through the new hole in the ceiling. Big Sal fired again, but the bullet hit the wall mirror, which disintegrated. Shards of noise cut ribbons in everyone's hearing.

Someone in the room above was pulling Pepper upward, gripping his wrists so tightly that the blood vessels swelled in the backs of his hands. Someone down below grabbed his shoes, but he slid his feet free and continued to rise, into the street-level salon of Cheval Cheveux. The noise of gushing taps swilled away any other sound. The torrent of water falling in his face stopped him from seeing or breathing. When the hands let go and deposited him facedown on the flooded floor, the dim moonlight showed him nothing but six silver waterfalls cascading over the sides of six sinks. Beyond the glass shop door were the agitated silhouettes of several men.

The gunshots had drawn everyone down from Le Petit Caporal bar above the hairdresser's. They were outside now, paddling, discussing why water was pouring under the door and who had fired the shots. When

Pepper crawled to the door, unbolted it, and tumbled outside into the street, an extra surge of water washed over their feet.

"*YOU!*" said Fléau, the recruitment sergeant.

Pepper looked back into the salon for the faceless someone who had pulled him up—but the shop was dark, and the sergeant was shouting earsplittingly about deserters and dereliction of duty, pulling out his service revolver. His latest herd of drunken recruits milled about, getting in his way. One was busy breaking open the door of the basement poker club, because he could hear people trapped inside.

Pepper ran. After him came the French Foreign Legion; the bouncer, bartender, and waiters from Big Sal's poker club; and a thin film of water slowly spreading like blood from the scene of a murder. He ran as he had run once from Roche, and even Roche's name chased him along the street—"Roche! Roche, you little bastard!" Stone chippings peppered the back of his legs as the sergeant's bullets hit the pavement. Big Sal aimed higher but was foiled by Mièle Rosette swinging her wet fur coat at his pistol and shouting shrilly, "But it's only little K.K.!"

At one point Pepper almost collided with a cyclist—
"Sorry! Sorry!"—and realized that his own bike was
lost to him, still parked outside Big Sal's. It was on foot
that he descended the steep stone steps, threaded the
narrow alleyways, crossed the canal bridges and ankle-
breaking cobblestones. On foot, in only his socks,
each lane was longer, each hill steeper. But minute by
minute he put more distance between himself and his
pursuers. Soon the loudest sound behind him was a
soft jingling and the softer hiss of tires on stone. Pepper
glanced back and saw the cyclist flickering in and out
of the lamplight, doggedly following him through the
small intestine of the night city.

It was Why.

"Why! . . . Why! . . . Bike! . . . Lend!" He was so
out of breath that he could barely speak. "Bike! Please!
They're after me!"

Why halted at a distance. "Who is?"

"Everyone! Don't know! Everyone!"

"Where are you aiming to get? I could take you,"
said Why, but came no closer.

Pepper gasped for breath, hands on his knees. Running had left him no time to think. Where was he

going? Home to an address Big Sal knew? And endanger Yvette?

"Could I hide out with you? At the loft?"

Why considered this. "Yes," he said. "Good idea."

So Pepper mounted up behind Why, astride the back wheel, his heels scuffing the road. The noise of starlings had long since been snuffed out by dark. It let him hear his pursuers, baying through the alleyways and the winding streets, as determined as ever to kill him. There was no moon. As they passed by the Constance Tower, Pepper looked up; but he could not see the flapping figure of a woman on the roof, the one who persecuted him so with her watching, watching, watching.

Suddenly he slid off the back of the bike.

"Where are you going?" cried Why, jamming on the brakes. He sounded truly concerned, and Pepper was touched.

"To ask her. Before they get me. I'm going to ask why."

It is hard to turn a bike around on cobblestones—the wheels jam between the stones. By the time Why had changed direction, Konstantin Kruppe was at the

240

far end of the side street, starting to climb the wooden scaffolding around the tower. He climbed as easily as a gecko up a wall, and the shadows swallowed all but the occasional flicker of shirt or hand.

Mouth open, head back, Why watched and held his breath. The noise of creaking wood, the slight tremor of the crude wooden scaffolding, made the whole building seem to be shifting uneasily on its base. Somewhere a dog barked. Reminded of Beowulf, Why turned and cycled away. He had been going to bicycle Pepper right to the doors of the police station, delivering him like a telegram into the hands of the law. As it was, the best he could do was report the whereabouts of the escaped prisoner Konstantin Kruppe and earmark the thousand-franc reward. As he told the desk sergeant, all the police had to do was wait at the foot of the Constance Tower until the villain came down.

"They're after me, blessed Constance! Everyone! What do I do? What do you want me to do?"

Saint Constance said nothing.

The Constance Tower is the last remaining stump of an ancient fortress. On top is a little turret that was once a lighthouse where a fire could be lit to warn off misguided ships. Unlit now, it had been no more to Pepper than a finger of dark pointing up at the stars. And at its domed tip, unreachable, the only sign of Saint Constance was the sound of cloth flapping in the wind. Here was no plaster statue, stony deaf. Here was the flap of a woman's dress, the same sound Aunt Mireille had made descending the stairs at Bois-sous-Clochet. Pepper had seen the silhouette so often from a distance, convinced himself that it was Constance herself. . . . Now he wanted some means of coming face-to-face with her.

He circled the lighthouse, but there were no rungs up to the dome. His legs were still shaking from the climb. "Excuse me. Excuse me! But why is it so important? I don't mind . . . I don't mind . . . but . . . but yes I do mind, because . . . yes I bloody well do mind! I don't know why you told me when I didn't want to know! Other people don't know! I wouldn't have minded then, I wouldn't! If it was a surprise. If it came out of the blue. I can't help running! I try not to run, but I can't help it! It just happens! It's like sneezing— you can't help sneezing, can you? I can't help running.

People shoot at you and you run, don't you? You would, really you would!"

Saint Constance said nothing.

Pepper sat down in the dark and hugged his knees to his chest. He knew his manners had slipped. He knew he was not being genteel, but how you do be genteel to a saint? You can hardly ask them if they're well.

Saint Constance said nothing.

"What did you die of?" he asked. "Were you martyred?" But the question only made him sound resentful and glum. Most of the martyrs got done to death in really horrible ways, but they generally had a choice about it. Nobody had ever asked Pepper if he minded being done to death. "You shouldn't have warned us. If you just hadn't warned us, I wouldn't have stepped out of the way, and you could've got me on my birthday!"

Crack, crack went the flapping fabric overhead, but the only other noise was the grumbling roar of some ship in the harbor being laden with salt. The town lights blinked out one by one and left only the lights of the Hôtel du Gare and city hall rising like the rungs of stumpy ladders, too short to reach the sky: Had they been within reach, he would have climbed them anyway, without a backward glance. How easy! Simply to fulfill his fate. Whatever waited for him after death, it couldn't be as complicated and tiring as this somersaulting from life to life, from bad to worse.

But Saint Constance said nothing at all.

The moon was late rising. The roof was pitch-black. He tripped on a baton of wood left over from the construction of the scaffolding and grazed the heels of his hands. Something wet trickled over his hands—it felt like blood, but his groping hands found a big can of creosote knocked over onto its side. It was while he was picking himself up that he heard the scaffolding scratching at the walls of the tower, creaking under the weight of another climber.

He could picture Big Sal's gangsters clambering up after him, the legionnaires with their rifles across their backs—"Head or heart, men. Aim for head or heart!" To these, his sleep-starved brain added Christophe the butcher, cleaver in hand, Gaspar the grocer, Jacques and Jeanne in their motorcycling jackets, the woman with the baby carriage, the landlord, the police, the navy and, of course . . .

"Father?" Pepper tried to think he had imagined

it: the grunt of exertion, the scrape of timber against stone. The high places were his sanctuary: Nobody had ever followed him up high before. "Who's there?" No answer but the soft sob of exertion, of someone climbing slowly but inexorably up the scaffolding. Pepper was cornered on the roof, and with so many enemies that he had no idea just whose hand would, at any second, reach out of the dark, whose face was about to appear over the rim of ancient, crumbling stone.

Where were the angels when you needed them? Where were the chariots swinging down from the sky? Where were the trench coated saints with their switchblade knives of light, ready painlessly to puncture his rib cage and let out the clamoring panic? His heart beat so hard that his whole chest quaked. His collarbones could hardly bear the strain.

"Go away! Go away! I'm sorry! I'm sorry! Go away!" he said, though his mouth was too dry for the words to make a sound. Around and around the little lighthouse tower he ran—a building no bigger than the funnel of a ship and just as smooth. No hiding place. He felt around him until he found the chunk of wood he had fallen over. He could maybe use it for a weapon to defend himself—swing it at whatever face emerged above the parapet—so long as it was not a flamingo or a horse. All the nightmares he had dreamed swirled like smoke around the Constance Tower, making the darkness even darker, making him cough and gag.

A hand groped its way into sight. White crab of a hand.

"Go away!" Pepper shouted, and swung the log of wood—missed the hand, but hit one of the wooden uprights of the scaffolding. A loud roar of fear was shaken from someone a few feet below—a man, plainly a big man with a rich repertoire of swearwords. Pepper struck again. Nails securing the timber slats to one another were jarred loose and tinkled downward to the street—*ting, ting, ting.* Like some big old wisteria wrenched away from a house wall, the scaffolding loosened its grip on the tower and keeled outward.

"Stop, lad! Stop!"

One more blow and Pepper might send it—some of it—crashing to the ground. All he wanted was time alone with Saint Constance! All he wanted was for people to leave him alone, to look away, to lose interest in him, to let him lapse like a forgotten idea. "Go away! Go away! *Go away, please!*"

The moon had cut its way out of the sea like a giant meat slicer and turned the mounds of mined sea salt to silver.

"I am not a great one for heights," said a voice out of the darkness. "The sea's more my level. I know I brought it on myself, dear heart. But I'd be awfully glad of a word."

THIRTEEN

SALT AND PEPPER

"Duchesse!" Pepper fell on his face and peered over the coping. "Are you a ghost?" The scaffolding was sagging away from the stonework, a crevasse of darkness separating captain from captain's steward. "Come up! Come up here!"

"God's garters, boy, if I move a muscle, this whole wicker basket will fall apart. While I accustom myself to the thought, could you tell me: Why the high places? Why are we here?" The scaffolding swayed slightly, like a tree loosened at its roots. Clinging to it, holding unnaturally still, clamped to a timber upright, Duchesse was frozen with terror. He was a man waiting to fall, defying gravity by sheer force of will. "Speak, Captain. I'm intrigued." His hair appeared to turn white in the instant, but it was just the moon breaking free of the sea, rising into the sky, its beams overtopping the tower.

"To see *her*! To see the blessed Constance!" Without looking away from Duchesse—Pepper too was willing the scaffolding to hold together—he gestured toward the lighthouse roof. He expected Duchesse's face to register awe, rapture, for surely he could see Constance up there in her blowing gown? Duchesse's face was a blank. So turning, Pepper looked up at the figure on top of the lighthouse dome, haloed now by the risen moon.

A flagpole tangled in a threadbare flag.

The mast top was round, like a head, but only a fool could have mistaken it for a woman, let alone a saint.

"Are you working for them, Duchesse?"

"Me? I'm freelance. Who would employ me, dear heart? I have messed up to some considerable degree. Working who for?" He tried to adjust his grip, and the timber sagged and shivered. The scar beside his eye contracted like the shutter of a lens. "Hades, lad, I don't think—"

But Pepper had withdrawn to the far edge of the turret roof. From there he ran full tilt at the lighthouse and jumped high enough to grasp the mullions of its windows. There was no glass, and the stone was thick, a handhold thick. The toes of his socks scrabbled for purchase on the curved wall. Luckily, generations of names, carved by vandals into the stone, had roughened its surface like a cheese grater. Scrambling up to the rim of the dome, he transferred all his weight to the dismal, ragged flag. Had he managed it an hour before, he would have been clinging to the skirts of Saint Constance. Now it was just a flag . . . and he wanted it all the more.

Instead of the cloth ripping free as he had expected, the whole flagpole lurched over sideways and left him hanging from the flag, legs flailing. Then the metal rod uprooted itself from its rotten clay footing and dumped him back down on the roof. A flagpole and six feet of crisp rag landed on top of him. He ran with them to the parapet.

"Grab hold!"

Duchesse shook his head. "You couldn't take my weight, son." His teeth were clenched so tight that the words could barely get out.

"No! Just tie the flag to the scaffolding!"

Being a sailor, Duchesse found tying the knots a

comfort rather than a challenge. Concentrating so intently on the task blinkered him to the swaying view, the gaping drop. He tied the filthy rag of flag to the wood of the scaffolding. Pepper, holding the flagpole, began to pull. The nails holding the timber squirmed in their holes. But the trellis swung back toward the wall, swung in, leaned closer, twisted . . . and began to buckle and to break up.

The upper scaffolding smashed up against the wall of the tower. Their foreheads clashed; then Pepper's hands were gripping the steward's jacket, while Duchesse grabbed anything stone, anything solid and immovable, slithering over the parapet, grazing all the buttons off his jacket.

Behind him, sagging joints burst apart; timbers and planks went tumbling, end over end, down onto the sturdier carpentry below, spilling matchwood slivers onto the cobblestones of the street, along with a hailstorm of bent nails.

"You could have waited till morning, dear heart, and come up the stairs," said Duchesse. "I think they unlock this place in the morning."

* * *

251

They sat back-to-back in the moonlight, and Achille Duchesse recounted the journey he had made, in parallel to Pepper's, that had brought him too to the roof of the Constance Tower. He did not make it sound like much, as if the detour had not taken him so very far out of his way. He was an old salt, recounting a far-fetched story to pass the time.

"Your father used to talk about you. Somewhere toward the end of the second bottle, he'd start complaining about the wrongs Fate had done him: harridan sister-in-law, a son not much rejoiced in for some reason. 'Pepper.' I was faintly inclined to feel sorry for said son—but mostly on account of the name. Pepper. What kind of a name is that for a lad?

"When you first came aboard *L'Ombrage*, I thought, *Roux's sending the son and heir now to do his dirty work. Apprenticing him to the coffin trade,* I thought. Or maybe this was a takeover bid: enterprising son snatching the reins from his father. By the time I got things straight, you'd waded up to your neck in it. My fault. My mistake.

"Then you started talking about going down with

the ship. Well. That was a . . . deciding moment, you might say."

Duchesse, unable to abandon both ship and conscience, had let the rest of the crew go without him and turned back to save Pepper from the suicidally noble gesture of going down with the ship. At the very moment the miniature Captain Roux keeled over from the effects of rum, *L'Ombrage* keeled over from the effects of scuppering. Grabbing up both boy and ship's log, Duchesse scaled the steeply angled deck toward the second lifeboat, only to find it jammed in its davits. If it had not been for Roche's stolen rowboat stowed on the afterdeck, the water would have closed over his story then and there.

He was struggling to unlash the boat when one of the fire buckets Roche had lifted down made a rush at them. In his effort to shield Pepper, Duchesse suffered a cracked shinbone. The Malay cargo ship arrived at the prearranged rendezvous and picked up the men aboard both boats. Its Malay captain (a disappointed doctor) confined Duchesse to bed with an elaborate system of pulleys to keep his leg in traction. *L'Ombrage*'s crew was quickly transferred to another vessel, but bedridden Duchesse and the unconscious little Captain Roux stayed aboard as far as Marseille.

"Couldn't persuade them to take the contraption off me, could I? More chance of persuading those damned parakeets to peck through the ropes. Result being: You left the ship ahead of me. All well and good, you might say," Duchesse continued in his casual, matter-of-fact drawl. "I hadn't exactly done you any favors—letting you get mixed up in the scuppering business. But I got to thinking: Where's he going to go? How will he manage?"

A boy with a good heart in the heart of a bad city.

"Soon as I was able, I went looking," said Duchesse. "Faint hope. Marseille is a big place."

Duchesse found lodgings with a pleasant elderly widow suffering from arthritis, and he spent a deal of time picking up dropped stitches in her knitting, filling saucepans for her, and fetching in logs for the boiler. Her name was Froissart, and she had such a partiality for walnuts that he never saw her eat anything else. For someone with arthritic hands to crave walnuts sounded to Duchesse like one of God's unkinder jokes. But Madame Froissart brought hers home ready shelled and insisted on sharing them with her lodger. "Little Pepper Salami at the Marseillais Department Store shells them for me himself," she said one day. "Especially for me, every morning! Such a dear, kind boy."

Hearing this, Duchesse put two and two walnuts together and made for the Marseillais Department Store. It was not simply the name that was familiar, but the nature of the act. Voluntarily shelling a couple of pounds of walnuts before starting a day's work—it bore all the hallmarks of Pepper.

Hobbling uphill, on a half-mended leg, to the Marseillais Department Store, Duchesse found the place in unprecedented chaos. Every cheek was pink from running, fighting, or blushing. Every display had been overturned. The floor was treacherous with olive pits and walnut shells. The delicatessen counter was abandoned. In answer to Duchesse's questions, the butcher at the meat counter suggested that if Pepper Salami ever showed his face in the shop again, he would have to carry his head home in a basket.

"I scouted about the city for a while," Duchesse recounted, idly checking his jacket for spare buttons to replace those just lost. "You had plainly moved on. It wasn't till I read Roche's obituary in the paper that I had something to go on. Then the article about the sinking. Strange thing, to read your own death in the newspaper. *A trip is called for, Duchesse!* I told myself. *A trip to this paper's offices.* . . . And I saw you, dear heart! I actually laid eyes on you!"

The streetlamps had just been lit in Abaron, and, along with them, new hope kindled in Duchesse of finding Pepper Roux. Thanks to Pepper's article, he was out of a job, dared not go home—might even be wanted by the police. But on seeing that small figure sauntering along from the newspaper offices toward the wineshop, he felt only delight.

"Roux!"

The boy took off and ran. Hardly surprising! What a fool—to call out the surname! What a fool, when the boy had made such efforts to convince the world Captain Roux was dead! Within a few steps, Duchesse was forced to a hopping standstill, obliged to watch Pepper flee down the dark alleyway, clamber over a fence, and melt into the dark. He asked at the newspaper office. They never revealed their sources, they said, And no, they did not employ anyone by the name of Roux. He asked at the wineshop whether the boy was a regular.

"Never saw him before," said the vintner—which came as no surprise either. After all, no one knew better than Duchesse the little captain's sobriety.

A finger of cloud had begun to scratch at the risen moon. Duchesse scratched at the stubble on his jaw. The stone beneath them was growing cold. "I remembered those prayers of yours . . . ," he said tentatively. "And you knowing the funeral service by heart. That hinted to me of a . . . ah . . . regular churchgoing." He trod warily: Sailing men could get very touchy at the suggestion that they were good Christians. "They weren't your prayers, I realize: the color of paper, the use of pen and ink. . . . But you carried them around with you and—well, that gave me the idea."

It was not the first time Duchesse had had the task of tracking down a wayward sailor, but the first time he had gone looking for one in church. Whorehouses and pubs were generally more the mark. But priests were almost as good as whores, after all, at knowing when someone new was in the area. So Duchesse got himself a haircut, turned up the collar of his coat, and became a plainclothes policeman, traveling from church to church, asking clergy if they had seen a stranger in their parish. He had read in the papers about a man who had escaped from a chain gang locally and was on the run. He suggested something similar about the boy he was seeking—a delinquent, a runaway.

At the candle rack in the Church of Saint Constance, he made such a miraculous find that his newly cut hair bristled.

"Reckon those plaster saints were on my side!" said Duchesse, laughing at his own absurdity. And he took out of his pocket the lilac prayer he had found on the church floor, and the ten-franc note, and handed them back to their owner.

> *Lord, now lettest thou thy servant Paul Roux depart in peace, according to thy word.*
>
> *Your devoted servant,*
> *Mireille Lepont (Miss)*

"You must've been there—right there! But of course I assumed you'd been and gone."

Duchesse had never thought of himself as a believing man—not until the fluke of finding that prayer, and what followed. He was hurrying, thinking maybe to catch up with Pepper on the road, when the priest, one Father André, came racing after him, apoplectic with fright. He told of his ordeal in the confessional: how the fugitive had cornered him there and poured out his iniquity—confessed to committing crime upon crime since his escape—murdering sailors, relations, and lemurs and rabbits. . . . It was all Father André could do to get his words out. It was all Duchesse could do not to laugh.

He could barely credit how close he had come to finding Pepper. And yet it came to nothing—that glaring clue—that divine shove in the right direction! Though Duchesse wandered the Camargue's wild places, the trail had gone cold again. The fluke, though, had lit in him the determination to find Pepper Roux, no matter how long it took.

The guise of plainclothes policeman had worked, so Duchesse found other disguises likely to draw secrets and confidences out of strangers. In Saint-Bonnard-de-la-Mer, while dressed as a nun, he was informed of a miracle at the local abattoir—a boy who had disappeared from mortal sight—probably plucked up to Heaven—when he stood in the path of stampeding horses.

"Redeemed the Lord's dumb creatures from bondage, he did," said one woman, tucking into a platter of rare beef. "Then got raised up to glory." (Funny how people's vocabulary took on a biblical quality when they thought they were talking to a nun.)

"Then my looking got me in a spot of trouble," said Duchesse, with an airy wave of one hand, though the scar by his eye puckered so tightly that it pulled the eyelid out of shape. He glossed over the next part of his story, wishing he could gloss over what had happened—paint it out of the picture and never have to look at it ever again.

In the middle of a torrential downpour—broom-bristle rain sweeping people off the seaside promenade—Duchesse caught sight of a figure running for shelter. He ran after him, his nun's habit flapping and slapping wetly around his bare legs. The two plunged into the same arcade of shuttered shops, under a leaking leaded-glass roof. The navy cloth he snatched hold of was bleached, frayed, stained, but to someone who had both sewn on and unpicked its naval braid, there was no mistaking Pepper's uniform jacket.

"It's me, boy! Don't run! It's just me!"

But when he turned around, the boy wearing the jacket was not Pepper.

After three or four punches, Duchesse meant to stop, to ask what the thief had done to Pepper, where he had left him stripped of jacket and money. But he found somehow he could not stop. From pillar to post Duchesse had trailed Roux's son, only to find that this thieving little hood had gotten to him first. "Did you kill him? Did you stab him? What? Did you?"

And suddenly the thief was lying crumpled at his feet, having answered nothing at all. A flicker of lightning above the arcade roof, the sound of police whistles, and Duchesse was sent flapping, vampirelike, into the public toilets to hide.

All this Duchesse reduced to a sentence or two, devoid of detail. "When the kerfuffle died down, I went back to my convent," he said, forgetting for a moment to keep his voice buoyant and bright.

"You joined a *convent*?" Pepper was hugely impressed. He had blended in with a lot of backgrounds lately, but he would never have dared attempt a nunnery.

"No, no, *chéri*. But I'd 'borrowed' the habit from their clothesline, see, and I make it a rule always to return what's borrowed. Jewels beyond price are the good Sisters of Troyes. Keep their doors open to strangers and their thoughts to themselves. Faultless on the hospitality front." Duchesse suddenly swore under his breath, recollecting. "But it was the feast of Saint Troyes, wasn't it? And the only sister who could drive a vehicle was in bed with gallstones. They needed a driver. Annual pilgrimage, see? Three-hundred-mile round trip. I had to drive them. It was a week before I could get back to Saint-Bonnard—to the hospital— make inquiries, you know?"

All the while he was chauffeuring nuns through the French countryside, Duchesse's mind revolved around only one thing: the theft, the thief, the jacket. Was Pepper lying somewhere, dead or dying in a ditch? Or had the thief simply filched the coat from a chair back or coat hook in a café? Or had Pepper swapped jackets with him willingly? Perhaps they were friends! Since

Duchesse had set on him, had the youth described his attacker to the nurses and patients at the hospital? Were the police making inquiries even now at all the local convents? Duchesse could not rest until he found out.

As soon as he had returned the good sisters to their convent, he went to the hospital, exchanged his habit for a doctor's white coat, and attempted to pay the lad a visit.

But Konstantin Kruppe lay dead on his bed, a sheet drawn up over his head, a lilac prayer on his chest with the added words *Rest in peace*.

Up on the roof of the Constance Tower, Duchesse said nothing of his feelings on seeing that boy-size body. Death, he knew, was very like a hole knocked in the hull of a ship: Nothing would stop an ocean of catastrophe from welling through.

The police were already at the hospital. Duchesse stood at the bedside of Konstantin Kruppe, helpless, appalled, aghast. A police officer tapped him on his white-coated shoulder and asked, "Can you tell us the cause of death?"

"Yes," breathed Duchesse. "I—"

Then suddenly a nurse appeared from somewhere, sniffling, saying her bicycle had been stolen from the rack outside. Duchesse simply slipped away, the lilac prayer curled so tightly in his fist that when he threw it aside, the words *Rest in peace* were printed in reverse on his palm.

There could be no remedy now—he knew that. He had meant well. All along, he had meant well. But, as the saying goes, the road to Hell is paved with good intentions.

He got out. Achille Duchesse got out. There was nothing in his mind but escape. Hitchhiking to nearby Aigues Mortes—a town far bigger than Saint-Bonnard—he went to ground. He was dimly aware that this was the home of Roche's widow—recalled well enough the address from all those abandoned letters of condolence in the captain's cabin. But he could not call on her—not her, of all people! For three months and more he had been trying to put Yvette Roche out of mind.

Nor could he allow himself the luxury of some respectable boardinghouse where the landlady would share shelled walnuts with him. So he hid himself under the fringes of the underworld: He was, after all, a criminal now.

A murderer.

Twice over.

Besides: This landlady could comfort a man in ways walnuts never could. All the sailors between Perpignan and Nice took their troubles to Mièle Rosette.

"Thought you were dead, honey!" Mièle said when she opened the door. "Read a notice in the paper. Someone having a joke, were they?" Beyond that, she asked no questions. She was fond of Achille Duchesse and glad to see him alive. From Perpignan to Nice, everyone was fond of the Duchess.

She offered to get him work as a bouncer at Big Sal's nightclub, or as a debt collector. But Duchesse only drew his fists into his sleeve ends and shook his head. He knew his capacity for violence now, and he meant never to let it out of its cage again. In fact, he put himself under a kind of house arrest, sitting in the back bedroom of the boardinghouse, reading the newspaper or staring out at the garden, thinking of Konstantin Kruppe.

And the other man he had killed.

Cash was a problem. He had parted with all his spare money, given it to Pepper. Aboard the Malay cargo ship, while unpicking telltale braid from the boy's jacket, he had pushed a roll of banknotes into the pocket—dirty money—money earned in the coffin trade, sinking ships: glad enough to be rid of it. Unfortunately, now he could barely afford another week's rent for Mièle. He put the fact out of mind. Tried. Tried to put *every-thing* out of mind. His tally of crimes was so long now, so haunting, that it was like putting a dozen cats out at night, only to have them come mincing and meowing in again through the window.

Opening the newspaper to look for an honest job, he saw the terse official notice of Konstantin Kruppe's death and gave a gut-wrenching grunt of guilt.

Glancing over his shoulder, Mièle said, "Well, look at that. The lies they tell in the papers! Little K.K. ain't dead."

He tried to break it to her that she was wrong—word might not have reached her yet—that this was one item of news he could say for certain . . .

But, "No, no," she assured him. "Little K.K. was here yesterday, right as rain. Came with a telegram. Such a darling. You musta seen him—no, you were asleep, maybe. Yeah. The telegram boy. Little K.K."

And suddenly the search was on again—like it or not—not a cool, collected gathering of intelligence but a rampaging hunt for telegram boys among the streets and canals of Aigues Mortes. It started at the telegraph office and ended with his kicking in the door of a loft apartment in the rue de la Poste.

Nothing. Two boys and a dog. But no Pepper.

Duchesse punished himself the best way he could. He called on Claude Roche's widow. No longer would he struggle to put her out of mind.

Or the fact that he had killed her husband.

As Claude Roche had raced, swearing, murderous, and naked, along the deck of *L'Ombrage*, swinging a bucket hook at the back of Pepper's head, Achille Duchesse had stepped from his cabin wearing a snowy *broderie anglaise* nightdress, and extended one foot. Roche had tripped, stumbled sideways, collided with a winch hawser, and pitched headfirst into the hold, impaling himself on scrap metal. It had happened so fast that he barely had time to cry out—though plainly there was time to call down a curse on the man who had tripped him. Duchesse could feel the curse in his hair, like guano.

Up on the roof of the Constance Tower, Duchesse brushed at his stone-dusty hair as if preparing for a job interview. He spoke nothing of the deaths, though they hung at the center of his life's story like a noose from a scaffold.

"I chanced to look in on Madame Roche—was passing through, you know?" he said breezily. "What likelihood, eh, *mon brave*? That we would both pay her a visit? Life is full of coincidences. That was how I found you in the end."

Somewhere a bird was singing in the dark, sensing a need to break the silence. An owl, too, came to rest on a sill of the lighthouse—round pale face, boggling eyes. It voided a pellet of undigested mouse parts: its own little explanation of what it had been up to lately.

"And you've been following me ever since," said Pepper.

Duchesse tugged at his hair with finger and thumb, as if debating whether or not he was in need of another haircut. "Here and there," he said with a shrug. "Now and then. When I had a minute to spare. Keeping an eye. Keeping things shipshape."

"Helping," insisted Pepper.

Achille Duchesse sucked in a tuft of cold night air. His coarse hair scraped the back of Pepper's neck as he looked up at the moon. "I hardly think so, dear. Making things ten times worse, certainly. Helping, no."

Big Sal's debt collectors were strolling along the rue Méjeunet, discussing what they thought of women like Yvette Roche, who threw saucepans at them just because they were beating up her husband. Grigiot was saying how saucepan throwing was the sign of a passionate nature; Pogue said it was a waste of good food and that saucepans were for cooking in.

Then they turned a corner, and a huge woman in a headscarf and tweed skirt hit them with a baby carriage. There was no child in it—only a pair of rope-soled sandals—but the experience was no less shocking. She went on laying into them with the carriage until two of its wheels fell off.

Afterward, she leaned over them, lifting each head a short way off the pavement by the hair, and snarled, "You bother those two again, beloveds, and I'll hit you with a train." Then she helped herself to all the debt money they had collected that morning, retrieved her rope-soled sandals, and strode off, dragging the carriage behind her. Its splayed spokes made a scraping noise on the pavement that set their remaining teeth on edge.

They pretended to Big Sal that Claude Roche had beaten up and robbed them; it would have reflected badly on their manhood to blame a woman in a head-scarf and tweeds.

"My trouble is I'm a rough man," said Duchesse. "Afflicted by spleen. No finesse."

Pepper could not quite make out why, but this sounded ridiculous coming from a man who was weeping bitterly. The steward's shoulder blades were pressed up against his, so he could not fail to feel them shaking.

"You got me out of the Foreign Legion, though," suggested Pepper, who had just worked this out.

Duchesse shrugged. "What? Oh. Yes. One of those kepi caps can be very fetching if you have a good square jawline, but on the whole I think you might have found the Legion . . . *stultifying,* dear. All that sand. All those flies. All that dying."

"And you rescued me from Big Sal's place."

Duchesse wiped his face with the cuffs of his

pullover. "Ye-e-s. I feel bad about wrecking that hairdresser's, but I had to do something to get you out of there. You went in blind, see—no clue what I'd done *on your behalf,* as it were, to those thugs of his. How sick was I when Yvette said you'd gone there! In all ignorance? Like a lamb to the slaughter? Couldn't sit and do nothing, could I? I asked Mièle to win me some time, but you were going to get minced, *chéri.* Steak tartare! So I broke into that Cheval place and turned on the taps. Put the dampers on Big Sal and his lovable crew. Hmm. I feel bad about those hairdressers, though."

They sat for a long while in silence, contemplating the accidents and mistakes that had brought them both to the roof of the Constance Tower. The owl revolved its head and voided another pellet, as if it were trying to teach them by example: Spit it out, men.

Why? (Pepper should have said.) *Why did you bother about me at all?*

Then Duchesse could have said, *Because you are the son I would like to have had but never will.*

Sadly, such things rarely get said.

Instead, Duchesse remarked, "I fear my contribution

has been one of two things, *petite fraise*. Either we are going to jail shortly or we are going to get killed. I seem to make an extremely poor guardian angel."

At which Pepper uttered a kind of snarling groan and said, "Bloody angels."

FOURTEEN

FOURTEEN

FOURTEEN

Pepper got to his feet. "Excuse me, but I have to get killed now," he said, whereupon he stepped onto the parapet. "I think you could say this is checkmate."

After a campaign as disorganized as the French transport system, the angels and saints had finally managed to corner him. Fate was closing in from all sides, in the shape of the army, police, gangsters, and friends. "They don't know you're up here," he told Duchesse. "Keep out of sight, and you can slip out after the door's unlocked."

Duchesse sat down sharply and very hard: an anchor trying to stop a ship from drifting onto rocks. "Get down, sir. Suicide's a sin. I don't hold with . . .

273

It's not . . ." But as the grains of soft, salt-rotten stone crumbled from under Pepper's socks, his words fell away into space, and he could not muster a sensible sentence. Only bafflement. "Why? Why do you always . . . ? Why so Hell-bent on this death palaver . . . ?"

Pepper looked down. The fact that he could see the pavement at all meant that morning had crept up on them. A horse-drawn van was delivering bread to a café. He did not want to land on the horse—he liked horses. He shifted around the parapet, the crumbly stone making a high, gristly whistle under his feet. Two boys on bikes were parked below, a dog lying between them. He did not want to land on them—especially the dog. Since there was going to be a delay, he might as well explain.

So Pepper explained to his steward about *le pauvre*; about Saint Constance and Aunt Mireille; about his fourteenth birthday and the bumbling incompetence of the angels. His voice was tired and irritable. The chase had worn out his socks: He could feel the stone of the wall through holes in their soles.

Duchesse did not interrupt—well, not loudly, stridently—*Don't be stupid, boy! Don't be absurd!*—

but now and then, here and there, he did make mild corrections in an undertone—quiet, pencil-light amendments such a the editor might have made at *L'Étoile Sud*. "No, that was me, Captain. . . . No, that was just Roche being his lovable self. . . . A note from the owners to your father . . . Illegal immigrants— that's to say parakeets for the pet-shop trade . . . A taxicab is easily hired, *mon brave*. . . . Birds are a little miracle, I've always thought. . . . People see what they expect to see. . . . People see what they want."

The boy on the parapet did not appear to be listening. But as Pepper talked and as he lived things through again, inside his head, the angels and saints who peopled the plot started to look somehow different. The drivers of fiery chariots switching on their taxi meters, the saints stepping out of the shadows, the angels hovering in alleyways and hospital corridors . . . for the first time he could see their faces in his mind's eye. And they were all Achille Duchesse.

Out of the blue, in the middle of describing the view from the roof of the Hôtel du Gare, Pepper screwed up his face so tight that it looked like the scar on Achille's cheek. Shouting with rage, he swung around to face

Duchesse. His heels were over empty space now. *"Are you trying to say saints and angels don't exist?"*

Cramp seized Duchesse in the calves, for all the world as if he were the one balancing on a parapet. "Don't be bloody ridiculous, child," he snapped, rubbing vigorously at his legs. "Of course they exist! How else would I have tracked you down?"

The horse and van moved off—*clip-clop*—down the street, the savor of fresh bread so strong that it reached Pepper and Duchesse, high up as they were. Delicious.

Duchesse reined his voice back to a restrained undertone. "But did it never occur to you, Captain—sir—dear heart—that when your aunty Mireille told everyone about her . . . her dream . . . well . . . she might have been *lying?*"

Pepper blinked, took stock of the question, looked for a true answer. "No," he said.

Well, he had to be honest. And there it was: the pattern woven into his fabric. If Pepper's life were a coat, Aunty Mireille and Saint Constance would have made it for him. His whole life had been cut out by them, tacked and machined together by them. His whole life had been fashioned by Aunt Mireille's vision the night before he was born.

Duchesse needed to stand up, to ease the cramp in his calves. He used the broken flagpole to pull himself to his feet. While he stood there, head on a level with the round, rusty-metal knob at the top of the pole, he wetted a finger and cleaned a patch of dirt off its round face.

"I like the saints, myself," he said quietly. "No dirty laundry. No axes to grind. Just waiting around to make themselves useful. No hobbies 'cept hymn singing and being agreeable. . . . Well, they wouldn't get the job otherwise, would they? Not if they showed a nasty streak? Like mine. Or if they hung around with vicious bitches like your aunty."

Pepper kept his eyes shut. He was bouncing gently on his toes now. A police car drew up in the street below. Stone dust from the rotting parapet sprinkled its roof like icing sugar. Suddenly Pepper opened his lids very wide. *"Why would she? What for?"* he shouted.

Duchesse winced, patted the air, watched the ancient stones crumbling under Pepper's instep. "Perhaps she mistook," he whispered. "I could be maligning

her—maybe she had this one vivid dream—mistook!—
genuinely thought—"

"*No!* She dreamed it lots of times! Lots of separate
times! And she said! She told us! Saint Constance has
very good diction!"

Duchesse, caught off guard, laughed out loud.
A big belly laugh. Roosting birds, pocketed by the
Constance Tower overnight, burst into the air now
in a single explosion of feathers and whistling. Pepper
was so startled that he almost lost his balance. Duchesse leaped forward, reached out a hand.

"The wretched woman was jealous!"

Pepper frowned. Having just begun to make sense
of things, he wanted to understand but didn't. "What
do you mean, jealous? I don't understand. Jealous of
what?"

"Of her sister, of course! Jealous of her sister having
a child when she didn't—wouldn't. God's crib, I know
I am! Me, I'd give anything to have had a son like
you. . . . If I were the marrying kind of man, that is."

Pepper thought. He flicked his way back through
the story of his life—the breeze of it lifted and shifted
the curls of hair on his forehead. He folded down

278

certain pages where Aunty Mireille appeared: her inventive cruelties, her busy timetables of Masses and confessions; the candle burns on his palms; no secondary schooling; hatpins impaling her prayers to his wall; her monopoly on godliness; her part in the ruination of his knees.

Pepper spread his arms wide from the shoulders, as if about to attempt flight—*"No, Captain! Please!"*—and stepped back down onto the roof. Clapping his hands together over his head, clicking finger and thumb, Pepper said, "Well then! What we need now, Duchess, is creosote!"

At the foot of the Constance Tower, several police officers ate breakfast at the pavement café and waited for the curator of the monument to arrive with the keys. Their pleasure in the rich black coffee was spoiled by a sergeant in the full uniform of the Foreign Legion, who was standing nearby, pistol drawn, and had been for many hours. All night, duty had pinned the man to this one spot, like a tent peg. At first he had been surrounded by a dozen new recruits, motley in African robes, dungarees, or Sunday suits. But they had drifted away, too bored or weary or hungover to persist with the idea of enlisting in the Legion. The excitement at the hairdresser's shop below Le Petit Caporal had stopped them from actually signing the recruitment forms. Looking at Sergeant Fléau now, they began to think they had had a lucky escape.

The sergeant was going nowhere. He had vowed to capture and execute "Legion Roche," the recruit who, in the middle of basic training, had defied his authority and made him look like a fool by deserting aboard a taxicab.

At a nearby table, Big Sal's "debt collectors," Grigiot and Pogue, competed to see who could smoke the most; the ground around their feet was snowy with cigarette butts. Billy, the bartender from the club, arrived and threw himself down dejectedly alongside them. Big Sal's poker club was a wreck, he told them—would be shut for months—and the firemen sent to pump it out had helped themselves to all the liquor from behind the bar. Apparently, Big Sal wanted Claude Roche sliced up thinner than salami. Those were his precise instructions to Grigiot and Pogue: "thinner than salami."

Astride their bikes, Exe and Why stood looking up at the domed peak of the Constance Tower, wondering if they had done the right thing, and what to do with the reward money. Beowulf lay between them, his twitching nose detecting hot croissants, beignets, and fresh-baked bread. Suddenly, a thousand starlings exploded into the sky and dispersed to all points of the compass. The dog sat up and barked.

A moment later, a figure appeared on the parapet of the tower and jumped off it.

He was wearing a harness of rope and dropped a yard or so, the soles of his feet against the stonework, his body skewed by the weight of the creosote tin hooked on one arm. Drops of creosote spattered the pavement below, like blood.

Sergeant Fléau, who had sunk into a kind of trance during the hours of darkness, discovered his pistol hand had gone to sleep and began frantically rubbing it.

"Klupp? Kronk? Krapp!" said the police, clattering their coffee cups, scraping back their chairs, hastily buttoning their jackets.

"Zee?" said Exe and Why.

"*Legion Roche!*" bellowed the sergeant. "*Surrender yourself!*"

"Hundred francs says he falls and kills himself," Grigiot bet Pogue.

"There's someone else up there," said the café manager, hastily making up his customers' bills for breakfast.

With a brush as stiff and unwieldy as a dead beaver, Pepper began to dirty the newly whitewashed wall of the tower.

"Bulls!" called Duchesse from the roof. "They love bulls around these parts!"

Pepper dabbed at the white rendering. "Bull can't read, though!"

"God's pajamas, boy, I wasn't suggesting the *bulls* would read it." Duchesse shut his eyes, dizzy and sweating. "We really will have to differ over your liking of heights, Captain. I cannot see the appeal."

Pepper broke off for a moment to watch the starlings ball, scatter, and regroup, making their huge swirling turns across the blue morning. And he realized that, for some time now, he had not checked the sky once for fiery chariots, meteorites, or black horsemen, for armored seraphim or the slings and arrows of outraged saints. The starlings looked too busy enjoying themselves to be omens or portents. He really did like high places. What had started off as sentry duty had turned into a pleasure.

"If I have enough creosote, I'll put bulls on the other side," he promised.

Early risers on their way to work stopped beside the café to look up at the slogan being daubed on the most revered building in the city.

"What does it mean?" said Exe to Why.

"What does it say?" said Pogue to Grigiot, having never learned to read. Grigiot struggled to tell him: He could tackle most words, but names were harder because you couldn't get clues from the words around them.

"Is he a Communist, then?" asked a policeman. "Name sounds kind of Russian. Konstantin."

His colleague bristled. "You don't have to be Russian to be a Communist, comrade," he said.

"A year it took them to paint that place," said the café owner. "Little vandal."

Sergeant Fléau said nothing. He simply flexed his gun hand once or twice, took aim with his pistol, and fired.

That brought everyone to their feet.

"What are you doing?"

"What the—"

"Who do you think you are?"

"You're not in Africa now!"

The sergeant, though his cheeks had flushed very red, was unrepentant. "The man is a deserter. In the Legion we shoot deserters!"

"Not in Aigues you don't!" said a gendarme.

"Not outside my place you don't," said the café owner.

Pogue and Grigiot smirked at each other. Big Sal had told them to kill Claude Roche—difficult under the noses of the police. They were happy enough to let the Foreign Legion do it for them.

Near the top of the tower, Pepper tipped the can sideways on his arm to stop the creosote from leaking out through the bullet hole. There was precious little left in any case: He would have to cut his message short, especially if he was to give the bulls a mention. The rope that ran between him and Duchesse creaked and shed a dusty green mold; it was, after all, the rope from the flagpole and had been exposed to years of weather: How much strain could it take before snapping? Out of sight, the voice of Duchesse remonstrated with him. "Get yourself back up here! What, are you mad? You're a sitting duck! Captain? Did he hit you?" But, because of the rope joining them, Duchesse was powerless to look for himself: If he moved forward toward the parapet, he would only succeed in lowering Pepper farther down the tower. "Look, sir . . . Captain, dear heart! Arrest is preferable to death! Get back up here, will you?"

Pepper began walking his way around the tower, lying almost horizontally on his back on the sweet-smelling air, looking up at the bright blue morning sky. And on the other side of the tower he daubed his steward's suggested message to the city of Aigues Mortes.

Down on the street, the curator of the Constance Tower arrived to find his monument the center of everyone's attention. A journalist had arrived from the local paper. An officer of the Foreign Legion was circling the building with a drawn pistol. A dog was cocking its leg against the fresh whitewash. The curator looked up—looked where everyone but the dog was looking, and read:

REPEAL HONGRIOT-PLEUVIEZ AMNDMNT!

Two police constables, their jackets buttoned up wrongly, instructed him to unlock the tower at once—immediately!—without delay! From the other side of the tower came another gunshot. Two telegraph boys, white faced and high pitched, let their bikes crash to the ground and ran at the gendarmes: "He's mad! Arrest him, can't you? Take his gun off him!"

"Unlock the door!" the policemen told the curator.

"Regrets," said the curator. "I cannot assist in the suppression of free speech." He only really meant that the police would have to unlock the tower themselves—he intended to hand them the keys—but then the Foreign Legion officer reappeared and, hearing the curator's words, pointed his pistol at the man and screamed, *"Communist scum!"*

The curator retorted, "I have that honor, you lackey of the state oppressors!" and threw the keys down a storm drain.

Big Sal's bouncer emerged from the other side of the tower, where he had been for much the same reason as the dog, and reported, "Bulls at twelve." Pogue and Grigiot looked blank. "Says on the other side: *Bulls at Twelve.*"

Exe and Why conferred, then cycled off in two directions, Exe to spread the news of a political demonstration in the Place Constance, Why to announce a bull run at noon. All thought of the reward money had melted away at the sight of the sergeant using their friend Zee for target practice.

Sergeant Fléau said he was commandeering the café as his base for military operations and told everyone to leave. The café owner told him to ride his camel up a drainpipe and not to bother coming down again.

Office workers on their way to work read the slogan on the tower and stopped to discuss it. A gendarme tried to play it down—"Just some little hoodlum holed up—on the run"—so they knew at once there must be more to it than that: The police never told you the whole truth. Grigiot, who had not been awake at this hour for twenty years, felt oddly hazy and began remembering his own days as a young hoodlum on the run.

"I planned on going to Oklahoma," he told Pogue. "Rustle cows."

The sergeant, on the prowl again, fired his pistol a third time. An almost-empty can of creosote hit a pile of fallen scaffolding, bounced, and rolled away down the street, bleeding blackly.

Up on the roof, Duchesse hauled Pepper over the parapet, and the crumbling green rope coiled between them like an umbilical cord. To the ragged grubbiness of the navy jacket had been added a hole and a dark patch of blood.

"*Now* can we give ourselves up?" Duchesse implored him.

But Pepper, eyes full of cloud reflections and the speeding flecks of starlings overhead, had other ideas. "Never say die, Duchesse!" he said, clutching the wound in his arm. "Never say die!"

Aigues Mortes was not as big as Marseille, but it was a *thinking* kind of a town. At that particular time, its bars and restaurants were always lively with debate—about the campaign in Africa, about immigrants getting French citizenship by joining the Legion, about Communism and patriotism and unemployment and the salt trade. This particular Wednesday grew into one of those clammy, oppressive days when the air felt quilted with salt and sweat and stale dreams. So when the rumor spread of a demonstration in the Place Constance—that someone had been shot—that the Constance Tower had been occupied—hundreds of clerks, factory hands, civil servants, and vacationing teachers hurried in the direction of the city's favorite landmark. Once there, they milled around, asked questions of one another, and invented the answers. True, no one could be found who could explain the *precise* ins and outs of the Hongriet-Pleanier Amendment. (Well, it was quite hard to read: Pepper might have gotten to grips with pen and ink, but lettering with creosote while hanging from a rope was still a skill to be mastered.) That did not stop people from thinking they had read about it in the newspaper and that it was a disgrace. Some said it had to do with immigration, others the campaign in Africa, some that it was a move to make Communism illegal. Somebody insisted it had to do with trade tariffs on salt. The police told them to disperse, insisted there was nothing going on—just some escaped prisoner hiding in the tower. So the crowd instantly knew there was more to it than that: The police never told the whole truth about anything. The artists among them mustered the makings of placards.

Meanwhile, those who had no interest in politics but did like thrills were delighted to see, emblazoned on the rim of the Constance Tower, the news of a bull run at noon. Why had they not known about it before? What was the occasion? Bull runs were generally the stuff of public holidays: Aigues Mortes loved them even more than politics. If Pepper had had creosote enough to mention the pope, he could have gotten the attention of the entire city that day.

"There will be no bull run today," the police assured them—at which the local bookies tapped their noses and filled their knapsacks with change. The police would say that: They were always trying to spoil people's fun.

The builders who had been renovating the tower arrived. They were enraged to find a section of their scaffolding lying in ruins in the street.

By ten, the Place Constance was awash with crowds. The lunch cafés had all opened early. Ice-cream sellers were cycling up and down, scoops strung over their shoulders like the boy David with his slingshot. Scuffles broke out between Moroccans and Algerians. Wine broke out among the local journalists who had gathered, scenting a juicy steak of a story. The police tried to break down the door of the Constance Tower using a bench from outside the Constanza Inn, but the customers at the inn made a counterattack to get back the bench and finish their beer in comfort. An African market miraculously appeared, selling fruit. Exe and Why cruised back into the square and sat astride their bikes in the shadow of the tower. To everyone's relief, the sergeant had disappeared. Young men combed their hair and loosened their belts—the first because they were about to draw the gaze of the girls; the second to let them run faster when the bulls were let loose.

Inside the massively thick walls of the tower's stairwell, the noise was nothing but a distant murmur.

"Why didn't Yvette tell me you were here in Aigues? Why didn't *you* tell me?" asked Pepper, sliding one hand over centuries-old rock as Duchesse carried him down the spiral stairs. Duchesse ignored the question, but Pepper just went on asking.

"I'm a wanted man. Unfit company. Now hush up, will you, Captain? Dear?"

"No, you're not," Pepper contradicted him. "You're dead. I announced it in the papers. You're as dead as you like." He winced as Duchesse came to an abrupt stop; he felt, too, the almighty shudder that went through the man and was instantly sorry. Perhaps Duchesse didn't think being dead was as wonderful a disguise as a nun's habit, a priest's robe, a kaftan, tweeds, or a red satin dress.

The farmer who usually supplied the bulls for bull running in Aigues Mortes complained that no one had told him about the day's sport. What bulls were they using? Why was he being slighted? He would bring his bulls anyway! Overhearing him, other bull owners decided to fetch theirs as well, though time was running short: It was almost eleven o'clock. Skirmishing had broken out between left-wing and right-wing students over the Hangriol-Pleuriez Amendment. The fire brigade was sent for, to turn their hoses on the demonstrators and empty the square, but (unaccountably) the fire brigade never answered the call.

Meanwhile, the recruiting sergeant returned triumphant, having finally mustered reinforcements. He proposed to storm the tower.

"And how do you think you are going to do that, then?" asked the curator with a sardonic sneer.

"With gunpowder and a fuse!" retorted the sergeant. And it was true. Sergeant Fléau kept a secret cache in a metal cabinet at Le Petit Caporal bar: gunpowder, bayonets, and smoke grenades to test the mettle of his recruits out on the marshes.

"The man up there is expressing his political beliefs!" bayed the curator. "He is Babeuf! Darthé! Buonarotti!"

"He's a deserter from the Legion!"

The curator mustered his full store of pompous authority. "This is public property, and I will do what I must to prevent damage to it!"

The sergeant responded by drawing his pistol again. The crowd nearby scattered in alarm. Fléau gave the command for his men to place the explosive against the door.

Legionnaires Mustafa, Norbert, Albert, and Nadir were boyishly excited. Caught between the horrors of basic training with the sergeant and the terror of setting sail for Africa, they were happy to be in beautiful Place Constance blowing the door off a castle: It was a schoolboy dream. Powder keg. Fuse. Match. . . .

"Legion Roche! Surrender yourself or face the consequences!" bawled the sergeant, his whole body arching in a rictus of triumph.

Mustafa looked at Norbert. Albert looked at Nadir. Legion Roche? Their fellow recruit? Little Legion, who looked about thirteen? Inexhaustible little Legion of the ready smile? Uncomplaining little Legion, who was named after somebody or other in the Bible? The boy who could conjure taxicabs magically out of the heat haze?

"We can't blow up *Legion*, sir. He's our lucky mascot!" said Norbert.

"Light the fuse!" bawled Fléau, the veins knotting purply in his neck.

"Flamingos is one thing," said Albert under his breath, and he picked up the powder keg resting against the door and pulled out the fuse. The sergeant pointed his pistol at both man and gunpowder.

294

Mustafa, finding a heroism he did not know he possessed, took the keg out of Albert's arms. Nadir, who had only joined the Legion in order to be with Mustafa, stepped in front of the pistol.

On the other side of the heavy timber, at the foot of the spiral stairs, Duchesse gently set Pepper down on his feet.

"Do you think we have drawn enough of a crowd yet?" Duchesse said.

"I never saw so many people!" said Pepper, as perkily as he could manage.

"Are you fit to run, *chéri*?" Pepper nodded. His steward, creature of many years' habit, wiped the door handle with his neckerchief before turning it.

Locked.

Sergeant Fléau saw the huge iron loop of a handle scrape a half circle on the outside of the door. He turned his pistol from Nadir's forehead to a three-hundred-year-old slab of timber and fired into it as if it were the head or heart of Africa itself and he the last true Frenchman standing.

Splintered wood and iron, bullets and noise, all

found their way into the gloomy stairwell of the Constance Tower. Then daylight, solid as a butcher's cleaver. The door swung open, the oil inside its mangled lock flickering with pretty little flames. Three people found themselves face-to-face. For quite a long time none of them moved.

Then Sergeant Fléau pointed his revolver at Pepper's chest and pulled the trigger.

For several seconds more, the triangle held: three people face-to-face. Sergeant Fléau looked at his handgun and fired it again. Surely only *one* chamber would dare to be empty, would dare to betray him? But no—indeed—after his onslaught on the big old lock, there were no bullets left in his gun.

Dauntless—possibly unhinged by the moment—he tried to step toward the enemy, to engage them in hand-to-hand combat—only to find that Mustafa had grabbed the back of his shiny uniform belt. Mustafa gave a pull. Sergeant Fléau fell on his back. Albert set the keg down on his groin. Nadir tied his hands with cotton fuses. Norbert gave Pepper a wink and a half-hearted slap on the butt—for good luck—as he and Duchesse stepped smartly over the pile of people in the doorway and plunged into a tidal wave of sunlight and noise.

Chanting protesters, singing ice-cream sellers, market traders foamed around the base of the tower, a spray of noise breaking from them that brought Pepper to a halt. The policemen had seen him but were more concerned with the keg of gunpowder just then rolling free across the cobblestones for anyone to lay hands on. The keg knocked over a trestle table.

Grigiot and Pogue had seen him and were smiling, rising slowly and smugly to their feet, settling up on a bet before coming after him, pointing him out to their friend Billy the bartender. Beowulf was quicker off the mark. The dog came bounding, wagging, grinning, slavering, thudding against Pepper's thigh and knocking him over—but only to get at the food spilling from the overturned trestle table.

Even with one arm still in working order, Pepper found it unaccountably hard to get up again. His limbs were heavy, his energy gone. Exe and Why saw him struggling and rode their bikes toward him, fencing him in to right and left with tubular metal and rubber.

Grigiot, Pogue, and Billy swung their jackets over their shoulders and, still chewing the remains of their breakfast like gum, walked their American-gangster walks, nonchalant and slow, toward the sinner on the ground—the one who had caused them to be beaten up by a woman with a baby carriage; the one who had trashed Big Sal's brand-new nightclub; the one they had been told to slice up thin as salami. From inside their jackets they drew out their delicate weapons— steel-bladed oyster knives as used by the best Parisian chefs. Cutlery was one area in which they were ready to admit the French excelled over the Americans.

Exe and Why ran in opposite directions, yelling like banshees, letting their bikes keel over, clash together, and intermesh over Pepper's head—a cage of handle-bars, crossbars, and spinning spokes. Grigiot and Pogue squatted down and grinned at Pepper through the spinning spokes.

Billy the barman didn't.

He alone appreciated that Exe and Why were not the cowards they looked to be. They had ridden in close to rescue Pepper, but time had run out and they had done the only thing sensible in the face of four large bulls hurtling, heads down, toward them. Toward Billy too.

The crowds in the Place Constance scuffled and scattered. Young men, fruit sellers, barmen, journalists, gangsters, and demonstrators screamed with fear or roared with sheer bravado, racing along in front of the bulls before taking shelter behind the Constance Tower.

Confronted with a bright, whirring pile of spiky moving metal in their path, the bulls peeled off to either side—a river of meat flowing around an island of bike parts—and galloped on in the direction of the causeway. All they left behind were their sharp, small hoofprints cut into abandoned placards:

HANGRIOT-PLEWIEZ?
NON!

Duchesse was slow to realize that Pepper was not close behind him. He turned back, swimming against the current, as people streamed out of the Place Constance, trying to get out of the way of the bulls. Meanwhile, Exe and Why had crept out from behind the Constanza Inn. Looking to right and left, as if for dangerous traffic, they returned to Pepper's side.

"Sorry, Zee," said Exe. "Very sorry."

Why jabbed Exe with an elbow: There was no point in apologizing for a betrayal Zee did not even know about. They no longer meant to claim the reward money; then again, they did not want to offer him sanctuary, either. There were just too many people *after* Zee.

One of those people appeared now. As Exe and Why wrestled to separate the handlebars and baskets of their interlocking bikes, a big, sweating man wearing a neckerchief came and stood over them. They noticed blood on his pullover, which was not heartening.

"Hello, boys," he said gruffly.

"Hello, Father," they said, freezing, rigid as their bikes.

"Borrow your bicycles, boys?"

"If you want, Father," they said—stick insects—invisible if they could just keep still enough. Duchesse did not look much like a priest just now, but the scar on his face was memorable, and the last time they had seen him, he had been wearing ecclesiastical robes and frenziedly taking apart their apartment in his search for "pepper."

"Obliged. I shall let you know where to retrieve them."

"Thank you, Father," they said, and Exe actually took off his cap as a mark of respect.

Pepper and the Duchess mounted the cycles—property of the Postal and Telegraphic Service of France—and rode away, Duchesse leaning across to hold one handgrip of Zee's handlebars.

"What do we tell the Kaiser about the bikes?" said Exe.

"Say the bulls ran us down," suggested Why. "Say the Communists threw them in the canal."

But Exe had had a better idea. "Nah. Say the Foreign Legion commandeered them for Africa!"

There was nowhere to go but back to the rue Méjeunet. A hospital might have been nice, given the bullet wound in Pepper's arm, but Achille seemed to have developed a loathing for hospitals. Also, Yvette would be worrying herself sick. Also, in an empty and derelict apartment across the street, Duchesse had left what little he owned in the world, guarded by an army of rats and cockroaches.

Anyway, Pepper was exultant. He did not care about the pain in his arm. He was alive and he was fourteen, and suddenly both things were allowed.

Aunt Mireille had lied!

What were the Legion, the navy, and the criminal underworld, so long as the heavenly militia was not after him?

Aunt Mireille had lied!

What did bulls and bullies matter if the saints were content to overlook him? The siege of Constance Tower was nothing in comparison with being besieged by the ranks of the blessed, and Pepper had just escaped both!

Aunt Mireille had lied! Suddenly everything and anything seemed possible . . . particularly with friends like Yvette and the Duchess.

"I wish you were my . . . family," Pepper said as they cycled. Not "father." He did not say *father*. As the word *dentist* smells of disinfectant, *father* was a noun that reeked to Pepper of drink and distance and disappointment.

Duchesse only coughed and replied rather tersely that "family" was something Pepper ought to be giving a thought to. His mother at least, who must be "waxing desolate by now."

"Oh, don't worry," Pepper assured him. "I wrote last week. I thought I should."

They propped their bicycles against the water fountain in the courtyard. The drowned sparrow was gone from under its rim.

"Aren't you coming?" Pepper asked when his ship's steward stopped at the bottom of the chipped stairs.

"I'll watch you safely to the top, sir. You get that arm seen to quick sharp. Sun's over the yardarm, I reckon. All's well."

"Where are you going?" called Pepper, but Duchesse was already across the courtyard and out of the gates. So Pepper turned and knocked at the peeling door of apartment 19. For the first time in his life, he felt that hand-into-glove, key-into-lock, wagging-dog, touch-the-mezuzah, hello-crucifix, supper's-cooking, place-at-the-table, come-on-in, shut-the-door feeling of arriving home.

Duchesse, who glided swayingly as a rule, and took his time about it, could shift fast if he wanted. He shouldered open the door of his squalid "crib" and snatched up a duffel bag. Into it he crammed such disguises as he had not returned, a newspaper, his shaving brush and soap.

Thinking he did not bother with. Thought he did not pack. Thought there was no room for. To his annoyance, he found that he still had Pepper's blood-stained navy jacket knotting its arms around his throat and pulled it loose: A ragman would not give ten centimes for it. The lilac prayers in the pocket? He pulled them out and leafed through till he found all with the name Mireille Lepont on them. These he impaled on the hook provided for torn paper in the water closet. Write home to that spiteful witch? Why? Why would you?

Silverfish infesting the floor of the WC shimmered around his feet, fleeting and repulsive as thoughts. He stamped down on them with a rope-soled shoe. Turning, he walked through a cobweb, and a spider lodged in his hair, like a memory. He brushed it onto the floor. No point in memories, remembering. Shelled walnuts or lit candles; Christmas decorations or death notices; letters of condolence with the address neatly written out in childish pencil . . . He had written home? To those unnatural, coldblooded, hook-clawed Roux reptiles? *Of course* he had written home. It was typical of him. Manners. Always the good manners. He was a boy raised by ill-mannered people to be polite. At home, Pepper had been the one expected to supply the good manners, as other children are expected to bring in the coal. . . .

"Holy Mary and Joseph and the camels!" said Duchesse; he dropped his duffel bag and slapped his head. He was down the stairs, over the broken baby carriage, and across the street in a twinkling. The stairs up to Yvette's apartment felt as steep as the sloping deck of *L'Ombrage* when he was carrying a boy in his arms. The front door stood open.

"Pepper! Pepper, lad!" he called. *"Did you put an address? When you wrote home, you didn't—"*

Number 19 was full of people. Not since the neighborhood children had come by for stories had the living space been so crowded. But whereas the children had settled to a wading sort of depth, the large men there now reared up like angry breakers over the heads of

Yvette and Pepper. The police were big Marseille men, but they were in turn dwarfed by the military police of the Foreign Legion.

When the Life Assurance Company was asked to insure the life of a man who put on the form as his employment "Foreign Legionnaire," they wrote back saying no thank you. They did not insure reckless idiots who voluntarily went to Africa to fight in a disastrous war, they said. (Well, they worded it differently, but that was the gist.) Thinking that Roche might already be serving in Africa, they sent a copy of their letter not only to his home address but to the administrative offices of the Foreign Legion. The address in rue Méjeunet was clearly visible in the top right-hand corner.

And that was how the Legion ran to earth the recruit who had deserted during basic training.

No such detective work was needed by the police. They simply received a letter from the Roux family telling them where they might find the notorious Skeleton Man, Captain Roux. They were ashamed (the letter said) ever to have given succor to a man who deliberately sank ships for profit. They were eager (the letter said) to help the forces of law and order track him down and put him behind bars.

In the face of all these people in her living room, Yvette Roche had become a silent ghost again, word-less, head down, dabbing a soft cloth in hot water, turning the water red. Pepper himself sat on the table, his face as white as any abattoir sheep, blood trickling down his arm, while debate raged over who should take him into custody. Everyone saw the cul-prit they wanted.

Well, people see what they expect to see. Or do they see what they want?

"We shall take him to police headquarters in Marseille," said the highest-ranking policeman. "If you people go through the proper procedures, you may be permitted to interview the prisoner in connection with other matters."

"Why waste everyone's time?" the Legion retali-ated. "We take him. We shoot him. We bury him. No lawyers. No paperwork. No prison food. Savings all around."

"Excuse me," said the Duchess from the doorway. It was not a polite interruption and was said with suffi-cient command to make all eyes turn to him. "Whom are we discussing here?"

"Roche. Deserter," said the voice of the Legion.

"Roux," said the police. "Captain of the merchant vessel *L'Ombrage*, sunk in dubious circumstances."

The *local* police were last to arrive. They came panting up the stairs now (already disheveled from chasing bulls out of a department store) and bottlenecked in the doorway.

"And you?" asked Duchesse with the air of a man showing superhuman patience.

"We have received information of the whereabouts of one Konstantin Kruppe—"

Those already in the room burst out laughing at the ridiculously exotic name—yet another name. The police sergeant at the doorway became suddenly three headed, for behind him lurked Grigiot and Pogue, the informants who had brought the police to apartment 19.

"Russian communist agitator!" Pogue piped up.

"We would like to question him concerning willful damage committed upon the premises of Cheval Cheveux, one coiffuring establishment, and for—"

"Terrorism!" Grigiot threw in.

"—trespassing at the Constance Tower, plus incitement to riot."

"He's also known as Claude Roche," said Pogue,

smiling at Pepper, sliding one hand inside his jacket to remind Pepper where the oyster knife was sheathed. The three kinds of police—military, Marseille, and local—competed to outshout one another.

"Tell me," said Duchesse, lowering his voice in the way that had quelled many a dockside brawl. "Tell me, gentlemen. Satisfy my curiosity. At what age can a man join the Legion?"

"At whatever age he chooses to put on the form," sneered the military policeman. "'S up to the recruit to tell the truth."

"Very well." Duchesse waved a dismissive hand. "The life insurance application: What age was on that? And what age must one be to make one?"

The neighbors, unable to contain their curiosity, ventured out onto the landings and into the courtyard below, arms folded, stretching their necks this way and that to see what was happening at Yvette's place.

"What age was Claude Roche?" inquired Duchesse. Yvette looked as if she might speak, but Duchesse forbade it with the merest lift of one finger and, pushing his way out onto the landing, asked: "What age was Claude Roche?"

The women only giggled with nervousness at being

suddenly the center of attention. So Duchesse leaned over the stairwell and called down. *"What age was Claude Roche?"*

Tentative voices called back, puzzled, uncertain, guessing. "Thirty-five?"

"Nah—older."

"Forty."

"Something like that."

"Thirty-eight, say. . . . Why?"

Duchesse pushed his way back through the crush of blue police uniforms, taking the opportunity to wrench Grigiot and Pogue backward by the elbow and, with a foot behind their ankles, tumble them backward onto the landing. Catching sight of them, a neighbor pointed and called out: *"There's those mongrels as beat up the storyteller!"* and the crowd gave a moo of agreement and moved closer, like cattle.

It was too much for the pair. They had been trapped in a flooded basement, kept up all night, knocked down by bulls, given the slip by Roche, and accused of assault and battery in front of two police forces and the Foreign Legion. They moved off, absented themselves, limped down the chipped staircase, and skulked their way—almost unscathed—through the herd of onlookers.

"And how long does it take to become a captain of the merchant fleet?" Duchesse asked no one in particular. No one in particular answered him, but eyes flickered toward the table, toward the ashen-faced, bloodstained culprit wilting in the airless heat. "Too hard? An easier question! What age is the escaped criminal Konstantin Kr—" The name did not quite emerge—as if all those spiky consonants had snagged in the man's throat.

But the police sergeant thought back to the wanted notice at the station: "Nineteen—when he escaped, anyway."

At which Duchesse banged the flat of his hand on the table. Pepper flinched. Yvette flinched. A legionnaire fumbled reflexively for his gun: He had seen action in Africa, and loud noises made him sweat.

"Then might I ask you, gentlemen, to take a look at this *villain*, this *reprobate*, this *sea captain*, this *insurance fraudster*, this *failed legionnaire*, this twenty-year-old *escapee from a chain gang*, this rabble-rousing Communist agitator, this demolisher of buildings!" Holding Pepper's chin in an ungentle grip, he tugged the face this way and that, pointing it at the forces of law, order, and military might. "I am intrigued, gentlemen. I am agog to know. Enlighten me. I cannot wait to hear your opinion on this minor but relevant matter. By all the saints and angels, *what the Hell age do you think this boy is?*"

Boots shuffled. Throats cleared. There was the noise of hopes deflating, doubts scuttling in like silverfish. And a host of eyes looked at Pepper for the first time with the express purpose of seeing him.

A small boy in his socks and an overlarge shirt, coarse, home-cut hair, and not the first sign of a beard. His boyish features were just starting to swell, as if childhood had only recently been punched out of him. A boy in the bosom of his family, sitting on the kitchen table, feet swinging clear of the ground.

Deciding to brush aside this minor setback, the most senior legionnaire said, "Sergeant Fléau will be able to confirm such details."

It was the turn of the local police to moo. "Fléau?" said one of the Aigues gendarmes. "The lunatic who just tried to blow up the Constance with a barrel of gunpowder? The one running around letting off a gun in a public place? We arrested him an hour ago. He's a maniac! Shoots horses on the Camargue—target practice. His own men said that. The ones who restrained him."

"A point of interest," added Achille helpfully. "He shot my son."

The legionnaires glanced at one another, starting to see—like a taxi emerging from heat haze—a scandal taking shape and speeding straight toward them.

The police sergeant's confidence was the last to be shaken. "You! Name?" he snapped curtly, taking out his pocketbook and wagging it at Duchesse.

"Achille Duchesse," said the Duchess, flamboyantly fetching out his papers from the back pocket of his trousers. "And this? This is my wife, Yvette."

Taking her cue, Yvette laid a hand on Pepper's hair and said, very helpfully, very sweetly, "I think a Monsieur Roche *was* a tenant of this apartment. Before us."

"And *this*, gentlemen," Duchesse said in thunderous declamation, "is my *thirteen-year-old son, Pepper, to whom I believe you owe an apology.*" And he grabbed Pepper's jaw again (probably to prevent him from correcting the *thirteen* to a *fourteen*; after all, Pepper was a stickler for honesty).

With the departure of the last policeman, apartment 19 fell quiet. Only three people remained, none of them related except by the lies they had told. The Duchess decided some social niceties were called for. "Permit me to introduce Paul Roux, son of a former captain of mine. I realize you've met, but I thought . . . to clear up any . . ."

Yvette reached out a hand, and Pepper shook it. "Delighted to make your acquaintance, Madame. . . . May I stay sitting down, please? I'm sorry about the smell. It's creosote. Mostly."

Yvette went back to cleaning and bandaging the graze Fléau's bullet had made on Pepper's upper arm.

"I was so scared," Pepper confessed, letting his head fall forward in shame.

"What's wrong with being scared?" said Yvette.

"It's unmanly."

"Well, *that's* all right, then," Duchesse said brusquely. "Most of the world's ills come of men being manly. They should try being womanly now and then. It has a softening effect." He felt obliged to add, as casually as possible: "I can't recommend staying on here. I've just shown my identity papers to the police. If they choose to check up . . ." Since the sinking of *L'Ombrage*, Achille Duchesse should, strictly speaking, have been dead (as Pepper had said in his newspaper), or answering awkward questions about coffin ships in a police cell somewhere. "And Big Sal's desire for revenge will be brewing up nicely at present. I feel we should all shift ground, if you can bear to leave such elegant accommodation."

Yvette and Pepper looked around them at the peeling paint, the fluffy mildew, the patches of damp, the holes begun by rats who had not even liked the taste enough to persist.

"I had a vacation once. Along the coast. In Garavan," said Yvette. "When I was a child. I liked it." She proceeded to write the word, in flour, on the scrubbed kitchen table: G a r a v a n.

Duchesse was slightly shocked, and insisted on fetching a spoon to get the flour back into the bag. But before he got back, Yvette and Pepper had blown and flapped it into the air—filled the room with flying flour, so as to let it fall on their hair and clothes like powdery snow. A possibility for the future.

"Papa's not in prison yet, then?" said Pepper, and found he was glad. Almost. Almost glad. "If the police thought I was him, they can't have caught him yet. That's good, isn't it?"

Yvette spilled over with indignation. "Pepper, he set the police on you! You let slip the address, and he sent them straight here. . . ."

"Oh no. That would have been Aunty," Pepper corrected her confidently. "Aunty always opened all the mail." The spoon Duchesse was idly twirling and somersaulting over and under his fingers came to rest tip down on the table. "*You* must be pleased, Duchess. You being such good friends with Papa."

The neck of the spoon bent. With the other hand, Achille Duchesse fingered the scar on his face that Gilbert Roux had made one drunken night with a broken rum bottle.

"Papa and the Duchess sailed together for years and years," Pepper explained to Yvette.

Duchesse could have added more information— how Gilbert Roux had gained absolute tyranny over his life. If he was ever arrested for sinking coffin ships (the captain had daily told his steward), he would be sure to take Duchesse down with him.

But Gilbert Roux was the boy's father, and a boy should not have to spend his life thinking badly of the man who begot him.

"Years and years, yes" was all he said.

"He must be hiding out. Like me." And Pepper, through sheer habit, began to worry about other people's problems. "I wonder if Mama and Aunty can manage."

The head snapped off the spoon altogether.

"I shall find out, dear heart. Write and tell you. Care of your local post office, perhaps."

"In Garavan," said Yvette, as if she were trying to fix the name in his head.

"You can tell us when you get there," said Pepper. "To Garavan." He could picture the three of them living together in a little house beside the sea. Interesting, but he did not picture himself going home to Bois-sous-Clochet. Not ever. The idea would have been like silverfish infesting his brain.

"No, *mon brave*. That I am unable to do." Briskly

efficient all of a sudden, Duchesse stood up, retied his neckerchief, swept up the flour, and returned the water bowl to the sink. A board creaked under his tread, and he rested his weight on it a couple of times more to find where it was loose. Then again, why mend a creak on a sinking ship? "I have to disappear now."

"Get a new name, yes," said Pepper. "It's easy. I've done it lots. You must keep Achille, though! Achille is a terrific name! I always liked . . ."

But Achille Duchesse was not talking about evading capture, getting away. There are things a man cannot ever escape, things that cling to him like hot tar, things that sink their teeth into a man's soul like a ferret's into a rabbit's spinal cord, and shake and shake him until all the sweet mercy of God and His saints is out of him. He brushed the flour off his pullover and with it the dreadful temptation to be happy when happiness was not his to ask.

"I know what we should call ourselves!" Pepper was saying when suddenly the scar writhed on Duchesse's face.

He snatched open the door. "I killed a man, Pepper. If you recall, I killed that lad Kruppe in Saint-Bonnard.

One dark and rainy night I pounded on him and pounded on him like some bare-knuckle thug, and a week later he was dead." The door slammed. A chunk of plaster the shape of a bird fell off the wall, and Duchesse was gone.

The starlings were as high-pitched as whistling kettles. They plunged and soared around the courtyard, weaving their trajectories in and out of one another at the speed of thought. Duchesse crossed the street, heading for the empty apartment where he had left his few possessions. His life would now fit into one duffel bag, if he could just leave behind all the bulky guilt and sorrow.

"No, you didn't!"

The barefoot, grubby children were playing with the broken baby carriage, spinning the wheels, folding the hood up and down. A couple more were riding the telegraph bikes up and down the road.

"No, you didn't!"

The cord of his duffel bag broke as Duchesse picked it up, and his swearword was like a hand grenade exploding.

"No, you didn't!"

Duchesse wanted to get out, to get started, to be on his way, but the door was blocked by Pepper Roux. Standing there in his socks, gray-haired with flour, the bandage unwinding down his arm, he repeated it over and over again until at last he had Achille's attention. *"No, you didn't. You didn't kill Konstantin Kruppe. He was fine till he ate the drugs."*

No one was more surprised than Pepper. Up until yesterday, he had believed absolutely that bloodhound angels had killed Konstantin Kruppe—had mistaken him for Paul Roux and sucked the breath out of him. Now, suddenly, understanding had lifted Pepper above the clouds, and he could see all sorts of things clear as clear.

"Kruppe stole everything. He liked stealing. Bedpans. Clothes. Curtains. He ate the medicine." Pepper scouted around for a charitable excuse for Konstantin Kruppe's kleptomania. "He was . . . he was . . . well, he was a moron," he concluded. "He broke into the drug cabinet and ate all the drugs like candy. That's when he died."

Duchesse set down his duffel bag and sat on it, cross-legged, head up, eyes closed.

320

On the way out of the hospital in Saint-Bonnard, the certainty scalding within him that he had killed Konstantin Kruppe, Duchesse had caught the sound of screaming. He had thought he must be hearing it all the way from Hell—a warning of what lay in store for him one day. But it was simply the maternity ward and the noise of women giving birth. A father, pacing up and down the corridor outside, with no one else to tell, sprang out in front of Duchesse like a mugger. *"I have a son! I have a son!"* Two, three, four times over he said it. And Achille caught a glimpse, at the back of the man's eyes, of something obscure . . . something rare . . . something like cartwheeling angels.

"I have a son! I have a son!"

"Lucky man," he had said.

And now *he* was the lucky one.

FIFTEEN
AFTER FOURTEEN

Back in number 19, Yvette pulled the newspaper out of Achille's bag and scoured it for names. But none of them seemed to suit. Duchesse was of the opinion that a name ought to be like a dress—simple, flattering, but with a little flare.

"I'm telling you," said Pepper, tired of being ignored. "I *know* what we have to call us."

They presented themselves at the Lost Luggage Office—Achille Aristophe Baron, Madame Germaine Gloire Baron, and Émile Pantoufle Baron—in search of the suitcases they had lost many months before. They had been to Madagascar, they said, and been quarantined after a spell of Lassa fever. It had left their memories hazy—unable to muster the exact details: of dates, of particular trains, of where they might have lost their luggage. But might it help to know that their initials were on their suitcases?

With a smug flourish, the lost luggage supervisor pointed out the three suitcases perched, like Papa Bear, Mama Bear, and Baby Bear, on the highest shelf. He handed them over in exchange for a signature in the book. If he was expecting a tip, he didn't get one.

Inside the cases they found their new lives. Books. Nightclothes. Shoes. Petticoats. A stethoscope. A box of chess pieces. An embroidered waistcoat. The photograph of a dog. A slice of wedding cake in a box . . . A few alterations would be needed, of course—a little adaptation to circumstance—but new lives, even so.

On the way to the station, Duchesse stopped in at a church to return a priest's robe he had stolen from the vestry. The light was lit outside the confessional booth: He could have gone in and confessed to stealing it. But now that the robe was back on its peg, he did not feel very contrite. He could have confessed to other things as well—he still felt bad about the damage at the hairdressers' salon. Then again, if the priest forgave him the whole lot—everything he had ever done wrong—total salvation might be just too large to fit in a suitcase.

The drowned Claude Roche would still beckon to him once in a while through the black waves of nightmares, but Achille could live with that. Rat catchers are probably troubled by dreams about rats from time to time.

So instead, he lit two candles—one for Kruppe, one for Roche—then went out and blew the last of Big Sal's money on a flamenco dress, by way of celebration.

They took the train all the way along the coast to Garavan, a little town within cycling distance of the Italian border. Cut off from the sea by the railway, its inhabitants had dug tunnels under the tracks to reach the beaches. Because who can get by without the sea slopping twice daily into their lives and washing out their mistakes?

Exe and Why received a telegram—had to deliver it to themselves—telling them where to find their bikes. They found them right enough, in rue Méjeunet; but having already been issued with new bikes, they sold the old ones and bought a sack of bones from the local slaughter-house with the proceeds. To keep Beowulf happy.

Garavan opened its arms to the Baron family. Their suitcases (and their names) gave them respectability. All three were hardworking, cheerful, and good neighbors in times of sorrow. These things are all a town really notices, though if Garavan had looked closer, it might have seen a happiness too large for corsets to contain.

Achille went back to the ships and endeared himself to a series of captains, using those gifts that had made him the best ship's steward in the merchant fleet: tenderness, invisibility, and superb scrambled eggs. The men he sailed with grew fond of his little eccentricities. He was a good man, and they appreciated him for that—though behind his back, they might sometimes refer to him affectionately as "Baronette."

Chère petite Yvette,
    We docked in Bois-sous-Clochet
yesterday and I took the opportunity to
make my inquiries at the hotel above the
harbor. It would seem the captain's house

stands empty and belongs to the court now. Unable to seize the man, they seized on the house instead. Rumor has it that Gilbert Roux took work with a South American outfit based in Santiago, shipping guano from that birdlime capital of the world, Nauru. Madame Roux and her sister (with whose name I will not dirty good paper) sailed with him. I have little time for the South Americanos. Many of the captains sail without stewards, taking their wives and families instead—an evil perversion of the natural order of things, to my mind. But if it means that Pepper's aunty must regularly visit the Kingdom of Seagull Droppings, I rejoice with all my heart. Nauru: the sky above, the sh— below. I have been there, and it is as close a place to Hell as the world possesses.

Tell the boy as much of this as you see fit.

Your devoted friend,
Achille

P.S. Excuse pencil. I have mislaid my pen.

In later life, Pepper also traveled widely, and he earned far more than Achille Baron ever did. He became a steeplejack, working on the construction of skyscrapers in Paris and New York, sometimes so high up that cloud vapor condensed on his eyebrows. He had always liked heights, and the work gave him end-less pleasure. The birds did not trouble him—except at lunchtime when, sitting out on the girders, he ate his sandwiches with a line of teetering pigeons pestering him for crumbs.

Some days he worked—death-defyingly—under a stampede of mare's-tail clouds, others amid magiste-rial castles of creamy cumulus, the sunbeams slashing through like God's saber. . . . But he never saw any angels or saints or fiery chariots swinging low. Of course not. As he well knew, the angels live quietly, keep themselves to themselves. Besides, they are tiny— barely visible. Oh, he had *seen* them now and then, but only cavorting about in the depths of his children's eyes, like swimmers in a pool.

Having a wonderful time.

Pepper died in his sleep at the age of ninety-one. The saints had gone to such pains to keep him alive when he was young that they were taken by surprise, and snapped their fingers in vexation. Some of them said that if it had not been for the Hongriot-Pleuviez Amendment (particularly clause five), he would have made it to ninety-five.

But then, people have a way of laying blame where blame really isn't called for.